THE
COLOSSUS
OF THE
THAMES
& OTHER TALES

A Steampunk Collection

MARK R BRANDON

For Harry

THE
COLOSSUS
OF THE
THAMES
& OTHER TALES

THE COLOSSUS OF THE THAMES

"WHO BUILT HER?"

It was *always* the first question when the Colossus hove into view as they passed out of the shadow of the immense brick warehouses which dominated this bend of the Thames.

Zachary Craddock had answered the question a thousand times and got exactly the same reaction each time. He sighed heavily and mysteriously. The sigh was a little theatrical, in truth, affected even, but this *was* theatre. In fact, in his humble opinion, his was a more challenging *metier* than theatre. Actors did not take questions from the audience, did not have to adapt the play every day to new circumstances. Actors did not face the prospect of the scenery changing around them or suffer the vicissitudes of the weather.

Zachary Craddock operated in a different class to those mundane thespians, declaiming, informing, *beguiling*, whether the deck varnish was crackling in the sun or the taffrail was rimed with frost. "Who built her, you ask? To tell truth plainly, my fine fellow, nobody knows."

"What do you mean, nobody knows?" The rough looking gent with the blunt-fingered hands of a working man spoke with the broad, gruff accent of Yorkshire. His eyes betrayed a fierce spark of intelligence. A Northern Radical, no doubt. "Where does her power come from?"

Craddock's eyes moved from his questioner to the queer cove sitting at the rear of the boat, whose gaze had been fixed on the Yorkshire Rad since they set off. Beyond the mastery of his craft, Craddock prided himself on one other – vital – skill: he knew his boat. He had, as ever, watched them one by one as they embarked, and the cove disquieted him. Perhaps it was the distinctly foreign garb, the green velvet topper banded with plum silk, the dark twill coat with the Crimean collars, or perhaps it was simply the copper spectacles with their dark lenses such as some brailler might wear, though clearly this gent could see perfectly well.

"So, are you minded to answer my question or not?" insisted the Rad.

He was excitable this one. Craddock looked to Green Topper again and made a quiet wager with himself that it would not be long until the Rad would be roused from his bed by the Peelers' knock and never be seen again.

It was a fair question, mind, though rarely asked this intently. Craddock wondered *why* the Rad might want to know. He fixed the man with his best stare. "That is a fair question, my friend, and most of you will have heard of her power, indeed it is something of a legend."

A boy piped up. "Will we get to see it today? Will we, mister?"

His mother made to quiet him, but Craddock dissuaded her with a wave of his hand. "No, no madam, your son is right to ask, for it is a spectacle most enervating.

The answer, young master, is that she demonstrates her power only when weather conditions necessitate. I'm afraid, to answer this fellow's question," he nodded to the Rad and then addressed his answer to the boy, "we have no idea where this unearthly power comes from. Perhaps we would have a better idea if we knew more about who built her, but we can but speculate."

The Rad muttered something about his lack of prowess as a guide.

Craddock had heard worse, but always met scepticism with charm, a technique which pleased the female members of his audience in particular. "Your eyes will tell us, my friend. Look upon her. Regard her regal bearing. What do you see? Do you see the hand of *our* forefathers upon her? The earliest depiction we have of her dates from 1075, but do you perceive Norman heritage such as might be seen at the Tower? Indeed, it is unfathomable that the Normans built her, having only landed in the country in 1066. No, certainly not. Saxon, then? They were a people of great skill, but to construct something of such immensity? I think not. Perhaps Greek, you might think, the twin of the lost Colossus of Rhodes? Unlikely. Her face does possess the grace and delicacy of a Roman marble, and they were builders of great fame...but her garb is not that of a Roman. Some say a visage of such beauty can only be that of Helen of Troy, but our lady here is most definitely a warrior."

The Yorkshire Radical looked dubious but had no response.

This was always the way. The question always defeated itself, and his blizzard of options only served to deepen the mystery. *Always leave them wanting more, Zachary my son*. So had his old da' said. The greater the drama, the greater the indulgence of coin at the end of the tour. "No, ladies and gentlemen, not Roman, nor Greek or Trojan. Yet where do we go from there? She has something of Egypt about her, for sure. See the distinctive designs on her shoulder armour – *pauldrons*, for those of you who are interested – they are reminiscent of Egyptian death masks and late period chariot armour."

There were a few low gasps then. The Egyptian craze had grown with each new gilded sarcophagus or crumbling obelisk retrieved from that frightful desert protectorate and conveyed to the safety of London.

"And yet," he continued, "little else about her speaks of Egypt. Can you imagine wearing all that metal in the desert heat?"

A few of the tour party laughed then, one of the various moments of reliable laughter, the perfect sweet counterpoint to the rich tang of mystery.

Craddock encouraged them to look up, then, as the boat puttered around the base of the towering structure. He never referred to her as a statue, that was very prosaic. Monument was more fitting, but it raised more questions than it answered, and an air of mystery could sour into profound ignorance if too many questions were turned aside or ignored. *Ignorance is bad for business*, his da' would say. *Speculation keeps the fires alive.*

Four times a day, every day, the steamboat would chug around the Colossus of the Thames, and each time, Zachary Craddock would declaim in similar fashion:

"No, no desert outfit this and nothing of the Arab in her. Our lady has the stance and proud nose and forehead of a Viking, while her ringleted hair and diadem are evocative of Celtic queens." More gasps, a few smug smiles from those who had been on the tour already and who knew this. "Her breastplate also has hints of Celtic manufacture, but the glyphs upon it are unknown forms and it looks hardier than their bronze plate. Her cloak looks fine, too fine to be the rough wool of Viking or Celt warrior-maidens, while the overlaid leaves of her skirt resemble the bronze armour of the elite Egyptian archers of the time of Mahamouset III."

Craddock paused, let all this sink in. He looked at the short Rad once more. The man was quiet but there clearly dwelt in him some nervous energy, a barely contained need. At the back of the boat, Green Topper remained motionless. The direction of his gaze had not changed either. The Yorkshire Rad was under observation, for sure.

"In construction she is composed of four hundred feet of an unknown stone which cannot not be chipped by any metal tool." Craddock paused to let this most remarkable observation sink in. The boat was wide eyed with wonder now, except for the Rad and the queer cove whose motives for the guided tour were manifestly ulterior. "Yet she has clearly been carved by *someone*, at some time. The who and the when are lost to time."

Just as well for my livelihood.

"She perplexes scholars and explorers alike," he explained. "Her greaves, for instance, were a complete mystery to us until the first merchants began to return from Japan and told us of the armour of the Samurai." More gasps now. The craze for all things Japanese had begun to surpass that of the Egyptian among the Middle

Classes. "Her feet, meanwhile, have simple sandals typical of Greek or Roman ladies, or any of the tribes of the Levant," he added, to add further spice to the broth.

"And her weapon?" The Rad again. "And shield?"

Craddock smiled indulgently at the doomed man. "Ah yes, the shield. My sources at the British Museum have revealed to me, after lengthy research, that this apparently mosaic'd shield resembles those found in the grave of Mixtec kings of the Lower Americas…"

The fog was beginning to curl in from the Estuary now, providing the perfect dramatic backdrop to his tale. Beyond the banks of mist loomed the dark towers of the Outer Docks, where fierce points of light began to emerge, picking out the tall masts of clippers disgorging or loading their cargos. It was time for the Colossus' crowning glory, he was sure of it, the moment which underlined that she was no mere statue.

"And the weapon," said Yorkshire Radical, "surely – "

Craddock cut the man off sharply. Nobody – but nobody – was going to steal his thunder.

"Indeed," he boomed. "Her weapon is perhaps the most telling of all, the most…*illuminating*."

They waited, rapt in attention for the most part. The sly joke prompted a few knowing laughs.

Craddock nodded to the boatsman in the tiny cabin on the prow deck, who activated the steamboat's luminal projector, which cast its broad beam into the approaching wall of white, throwing light over the lower part of the Colossus.

"Note, if you will, this spear she holds, and its trifurcated point." Would it happen, this time? With the changing climate, the incidences had lessened, but the augurs were good today, for it was both cold and humid and the Estuary fog was thickening. He pulled his thick coat tighter, let the fur collar wrap his neck.

Did he see a flicker then, the almost imperceptible sign that something wondrous would occur? They may all have seen it, from a distant hill, but up close, it was thrilling beyond imagining. And he, master craftsman, was able to time the end of his presentation to its appearance.

"This can only mean one thing." He let the last syllable linger on his tongue.

There was the flicker again, for sure this time, a tiny white spark between two prongs of her forked spear.

"The trifurcated spear, the untranslatable forms, the strange armour of such delicate beauty."

There was a third flicker. Now. It was now.

"The Colossus of the Thames," he declaimed triumphantly, "can only be...the *Queen of Atlantis*!"

The tour party gasped as light exploded from the spear, precisely on cue, in three titanic beams. One was directed towards each shore and one out to sea, so that the Colossus of the Thames might guide her adopted children home, to the mystical capital of the world, the centre of learning and culture and hub of the greatest city on Earth.

The Rad's mouth fell open. Green Topper remained perfectly still, oblivious to the spectacle, instead watching the Rad.

Craddock felt tears come to his eyes, as they always did when the beams appeared.

It was her crowning achievement, her function, her *magic*.

And he, he was her self-appointed steward, her most devoted acolyte.

"God save the Queen," he whispered, treasonously.

ΨΨΨΨΨΨ

THE STRANGE CASE OF THE EMERALD NECKLACE

"GOOD LORD, MAN, you can't possibly mean…?"

"Yes, my dear Marquis, there can only be one possible solu…"

The abrupt halt became a pause and threatened to develop into a hiatus.

The Marquis of Steeltown Rashes shifted uncomfortably in the battered leather wingback chair. Outside on the street, the paperboys were declaiming another great victory on the shores of the Black Sea.

He risked a polite cough.

The detective remained utterly motionless.

"One possible *solution*?" said the Marquis.

The detective leapt into life. "…tion!"

"Yes?"

"Only the Marchioness could have taken the emerald necklace!"

"You can't be serious?" spluttered the Marquis, though it was, secretly, exactly as he had feared all this time.

The room rattled as the Pneumatic Underground train from Paddington Overground to Waterloo-Gare des Dirigeables rumbled through underneath the building.

"Yes!" cried the detective, excitably. "She knew nobody would suspect. She took Colonel Blimpington's monocle when he placed it on the side of the billiard table to adjust his shot. She then used it to burn a hole in Madame De Rochefoucauld's crinoline, and in the mayhem which ensued, the Marchioness took the emerald necklace from the fainted Contessa and hid it in the ostrich head, knowing full well nobody would ever look there. The blind ornithologist had seen to that!"

"Dear God." The Marquis fluttered one doeskin glove in front of his face.

"For your wife, my good sir, is none other than…"

"Yes?"

The detective went perfectly still.

"Oh!" said the Marquis. He heard a faint click, then a 'clunk'.

That did not sound good…

The nobleman rose from his chair and went to the detective. "Oh dear." He put his gloves back on and poked experimentally at the detective with one slim finger. Nothing. "Oh, dear oh dear oh dear oh dear."

The Marquis looked around the shabby room for something which might help. The grate held a fine poker set, each utensil capped with a brass double-headed eagle. *That will never do.* He looked at the mantelshelf. Next to a faded daguerreotype of Alexandrina The Forever Queen lay a brass handle. Was that the thing? He was quite hopeless with this sort of affair. His was the world of *salon* conversation, of poetry readings and piano recitals and costume balls not base *tinkering*. The clue was in the word – *tinker*. What was he, some kind of rag-and-bone man expected to pluck the correct tool from a selection of oily implements?

"Damfino!" he cursed. It was his new favourite word, acquired in Mme De Bourbon's enchanting Holland Park company, and now employed almost to excess, not least because nobody in his circle had the faintest clue what it meant. He didn't either, beyond its deliciously scandalous suggestion of the word 'damn'.

The Marquis picked up the handle anyway, looked at it as if it were a stick of dynamite he could not let go of, then fluttered about, poking papers, examining cluttered surfaces, peering into jars and even opening a drawer or two to see if he could find anything to demonstrate its correct usage. He sighed loudly, then suddenly realised there was another presence in the room. He turned around to see the detective's housekeeper standing in the doorway. "Damfino!"

"Oh, begging your pardon, sir, I'm sure." The woman's tone was uncertain, perhaps slightly suspicious.

"I…er…"

"Can I be of assistance?" The prim, middle-aged woman smoothed the front of her pinafore dress, then made to adjust her mobcap. She was looking determinedly at the brass handle.

The Marquis looked at her and then at the handle.

"You didn't…?" She raised a quizzical eyebrow.

The Marquis stared at her and then at the handle and felt himself flush. "No, gracious!" he exclaimed, finally fitting the puzzle pieces together. "I merely picked up this handle as a curiosity, wondering if it might be of some use.

The detective was engaged in a most revelatory discourse and then…"

"Yes, sir?" Her stare had softened a little, but only a little, and the eyebrow remained raised.

"Well, he simply…ceased." The Marquis shrugged his shoulders, proferred the handle. "I am extremely desirous to learn what he was about to impart."

"Was he agitated?" The housekeeper glanced again at the handle. "You haven't been *winding him up*, have you?"

"Oh, gracious, no." The Marquis looked at the handle as if it were a poisonous snake, then felt in his waistcoat pocket for a handkerchief to mop his brow. "But it did feel as though he himself was getting a little, er, wound up, as you say."

"Ah." The housekeeper's eyebrow finally returned to its starting position. "That'll be it then, sir. This often happens I'm afraid."

"Does it?"

"Yes." She moved to the detective, took up her apron and polished an imaginary smudge on his brass cheek. "It'll be his mainspring, you see. Sometimes he gets a little wound up all on his own, especially when he's expounding the solution to a mystery."

"Ah," said the Marquis.

"We need to let him wind down a bit," said the housekeeper. "I'm sure he'll be right as rain in an hour or so. Would you like some tea? I have some made from a Peruvian leaf which has a pleasingly calmative effect."

"That would be wonderful."

The housekeeper showed him out and motioned him towards the drawing room.

In the front lounge, Clockwork Holmes, the Great Brass Detective, clicked and whirred, slowly regaining his poise.

ΨΨΨΨΨΨ

THE NIGHT DOCTOR

SUDDENLY, THERE CAME a sharp rap at the front door. The Doctor looked up from his ministrations. This could not possibly be another visitor for Mrs Engels, not at this time of night. He looked at her. She did not stir. The sedative had done the trick. He heard the maid shuffling down the corridor in her slippers to the doorway and began to pack up his bag.

The maid opened the hefty front door. "Yes?" she snapped.

The Doctor winced at the tone. He supposed Louisa would feel that three o'clock in the morning was no time for visitors of any kind. Her frosty expression when she had opened the door to him an hour earlier had certainly left him in no doubt as to her opinion of her mistress's latest call to the Night Doctor.

"I'm so sorry to bother you at this hour, miss," came the voice from outside, its Irish accent immediately recognisable.

The Doctor's heart quickened. It was much as he had feared.

"Yes, it is a late hour for bother!" said the maid.

"Begging your pardon, miss, but is the Doctor there?"

The Doctor, bag in hand, promptly entered the hallway. "I am here, Vincent."

"Ah," said the lad. "I've a Hansom waiting."

"Well," said the maid, "this is somewhat irregular!"

The Doctor turned to her, clasped both her hands and smiled, affecting his best bedside manner. "I have another call, Louisa. Your mistress will be fine, I assure you. I have left some powders for her. Make sure she takes one in the morning after breakfast and one in the evening after dinner, both times with plenty of water. Keep her off the sherry and call me if the condition recurs. I think she will be right as rain in a few days. I'll have my man here bring around my invoice for her kind attention once she has recovered."

The maid was duly disarmed. "Oh, well. Right enough. I'll look after her, sir."

"I have every faith in you." The Doctor smiled unctuously.

He stepped down into the street where Vincent held open the door to the Automatic Cabriolet. The driver sat perfectly motionless atop it, its brass half-face catching the amber light from the gas lamp outside the house. When they sent for him, it was always an Automatic. Automatics told no tales.

The lad fed an ivory punch-card into the destination slot and the driver's head rose, its headlamps illuminated, pointing straight ahead into the night. Once in the cab, Vincent hit the large black gutta percha button labelled 'GO!'

The Doctor breathed a heavy sigh. "Is it…?"

"I'm afraid so."

"Bayswater, I take it," said the Doctor.

"Yes, sir, I'm afraid so."

The Doctor sighed. "Thank you, Vincent, your assistance is invaluable."

"That's perfectly alright." The lad sat back and stretched his arms out, stifled a yawn.

Vincent was an uncanny fit for the Doctor – physically strong, highly organised and with a broad network of useful connections. During their two-year acquaintance, since he had turned up at the surgery seeking gainful employment, the Doctor had found that Vincent possessed other useful traits, one in particular which made their task a lot easier.

For behind his good looks lay a cold, *cold* heart. In fact, the lad seemed to possess no finer feeling whatever for his fellow man. Whether this had been a result of witnessing the slaughtering of lambs and piglets on the farm where he'd been raised, or whether it was simply a heritable trait, such as that espoused in all the latest scientific literature, the Doctor could not be sure. With education, Vincent might have made a fine surgeon, the Doctor thought. Surgeons were required to be thoroughly detached from the consequences of their actions, in emotional terms, and Vincent was certainly detached. Many a broken-hearted flower girl could attest to that. He was a veritable *beast*.

"Did you...?" started the Doctor, unnecessarily.

Vincent smiled wolfishly. "Yeah, I telegraphed to Kentish Town, told Joe and the lads to meet us there."

The Doctor's heart sank. The crew's attendance at least relieved him of some of the more unpleasant aspects of his job, but the need for their presence indicated this was a bad one. Telegraph in the middle of the night was a gut-wrenchingly expensive action, but this was one of those 'no expenses spared' assignments.

They did not always require his appearance. Sometimes only the clean-up crew was required. For the Doctor to be called personally meant there was a *situation* of some delicacy. Usually the same situation, mind, which did not speak favourably of his clients' care or attention during the course of their activities. "Did you…?"

"Bring your special bag?" Vincent smiled. "Of course, Doctor. You know you can always rely on me."

The Doctor nodded. It was true, he could. Despite all being in order, his anxiety worsened as the Hansom trotted on towards Bayswater. Not wishing to look at Vincent's troubling smile, he gazed out of the window of the cab where gas lamps flicked by blurrily above the shining pavement.

As the cab turned into *that* street, he felt a knot in his stomach. They trotted on until they were outside Number Fourteen.

That house.

The house itself was grand, but unremarkable, a white stucco'd four storey townhouse in a row of identical houses, facing another row of the same. Five deep steps led up to a pillared porch and shiny black door with regulation brass numbers and regulation brass knocker and knob, the door furniture perfectly identical to that which adorned every other door in the street.

An identical house in a nonesuch street which did not feature on any policeman's patrol-route nor on any street-map available for public purchase. The street itself was a dead end so nor would there be any passers-by. Nor would tradesmen ever bother the denizens of the street, because said denizens never needed anything, except occasionally his good self. Should any poor wretch wander by mistake into the street, they would not be aware that Number Fourteen was the only one of the fifty-six houses on the street which was actually occupied.

Perfect anonymity.

They dismounted the cab. Vincent pre-paid the return fare and set the cab to WAIT. The driver's headlamps turned off.

Joe and his clean-up crew sat quietly on the other side of the road next to their steam-wagon. It looked for all the world like a billposter's cart, an ill-favoured, dusty thing with a scratched black boiler and crowned stack, a very dated feature these days. Its sides were drab, unrevealing. It was the perfect disguise for this benighted charnel-wagon.

"Alright Doctor?" Joe puffed a great cloud of smoke into the air. His three lads all chuckled conspiratorially, suddenly competing with one another as to who could force the largest smoke-cloud from their lungs. One of them fell to coughing and got a sharp rap on the head with Joe's hunting stick for his trouble. It did not stop him coughing, but at least he would aim to do it more quietly.

The Doctor realised he had been holding his breath. It was surpassingly unlikely they would be disturbed on this street, at this time, but you could not be too careful. Oh, they would be able to buy off one policeman, surely, but two? More problematic. Vincent had said that one time, on a call when the Doctor had not been required, a young policeman had wandered into the street and questioned Joe. He had been 'cleaned-up', which then required some further cleaning up at Scotland Yard, involving a personage of distinction who had made it emphatically clear that such a foul error should never – repeat *never* – be repeated.

The Doctor nodded curtly towards Joe. The bruiser laughed gently in response and may even have winked, though that could have been a trick of the light. The Doctor gathered up his special case and made his way up the stairs to the front door. Now he felt nauseated, tense with anxiety. His bowels turned over like a cabbage dropped in a bucket of ice water.

He knocked at the door, once, twice, three times, firmly but gently so as to make an appropriate, but discreet, amount of noise.

He waited.

Perhaps ten seconds later, the door swung open, seemingly of its own volition. He gulped and both he and Vincent stepped inside. The door swung closed behind them, and they heard a dull click as it closed.

The Doctor reeled. He had entirely forgotten to apply camphorated balm to his nostrils and upper lip, and nearly gagged. Vincent tapped him on the elbow and passed him the small white porcelain jar. The lad was still smiling. *How could he?*

The tang of the gummy balm began to mitigate the foul stench which permeated the house. The Doctor shuddered and looked around. The wide hallway seemed even more dishevelled than it had done on his last visit. It had been richly decorated at some point, but the black silk damask adorning the walls was grubby and torn to head height, its gold fleur-de-lis imprint barely visible except near the ceiling, such was the fading, scuffing and extensive staining on the larger part of the walls. The elegant pattern on the tiled floor was barely visible under a layer of grime. The floor was, as usual, faintly sticky. Two grand brass wall lamps, both in need of a good polish, provided a greasy yellow light.

They moved down the hallway, past the foot of the stairs, past the front room and drawing room, whence came faint gramophone music, past the dining room and towards the kitchens at the rear of the house. The smell threatened to break through the balm, and the Doctor reapplied, his eyes tearing up.

A man stood in the doorway to the kitchen under a chandelier, smiling as they approached. He was perhaps fully six feet tall, of slim build. He was gaunt of face, with taut, filthy parchment skin, topaz eyes glimmering in the flickering light and wore his dirty blond hair long, with a woven 'rat-tail' over each ear, the so-called 'Bohemian' style, as had been the brief vogue among artists and other wasters perhaps five years ago. He was dressed in an expensive linen suit and stained black boots and carried a stick of dark wood topped with a golden dragon emblem. Several necklaces of gold, bone and wood crowned a pallid, bony chest, visible through the open collars. Copious amounts of fresh blood disguised a cresting of gold rings on both hands. The cuffs of the expensive shirt were drenched with gore while the pale suit was spattered extravagantly with the same, and the left leg bore a more significant stain studded with gobbets of torn flesh.

"Dimonius," said the Doctor, without inflection.

"Well met, Doctor."

"It seems as if you have had a…*busy* night." Behind the Doctor, Vincent tutted.

Dimonius threw his head back and laughed. It was not a pleasant sound, rather a bubbling, gurgling noise which chilled the Doctor to hear. "Yes, you might say that, although I do wish you'd try harder to disguise the disgust in your voice. It does you no credit."

The Doctor could never place Dimonius' accent, in fact tried not to think of it at all when he was outside of this Pit of Infernus. "Where is…she, I take it?"

Dimonius laughed. "Actually, Doctor, tonight it is a *boy* who is in need of your, ahem, special ministrations."

Vincent growled.

"A boy," said the Doctor, somewhat relieved. It was easier with boys. The last had been a girl, a girl who had filled his nightmares for weeks afterwards.

"I shall take you to him." Dimonius picked up his stick and strolled past the Doctor and Vincent on his way to the stairs. As he passed, Vincent's lip curled.

They mounted the stairs quickly, Dimonius prancing ahead like some kind of imp. The Doctor presumed it amused him, this affected jig of a walk. Dimonius was always the showman. The Doctor recalled having met him in daylight only once, at dusk, in St James's Park. Dimonius had appeared in a lavender suit of the most luxurious twill adorned with twisted cord at lapels, pockets and cuffs, pale lavender gloves and a shiny black cane capped with a silver ostrich head. A grey velvet top hat sat upon a full head of lustrous grey hair. The creature regarded the Doctor with wry amusement from behind a preposterous pair of spectacles with pink, octagonal lenses. Dimonius had insisted on performing card tricks for a gaggle of young girls from one of the less renowned private schools, and then upon buying them Italian ice from a vendor's cart when he was done. The Doctor felt ill throughout the whole encounter, wondering how and when Dimonius would arrange to have the girls taken. Seeing his discomfiture, Dimonius had taken a fat manila envelope from his jacket pocket and curled the Doctor's hand around it, stilling any thought of comment or, worse, rebellion.

They reached the top of the stair and Dimonius led them into the upstairs drawing room. This was the regular location for his work, so the Doctor barely looked at the lavish Turkish couches, the Ormulu clocks on the mantel or magnificent Queen Anne sideboard. Nor did he pay much attention to the four figures in various stages of undress, who lay slumped on the couches or the large Chinese floor cushions. Instead, he made for the stiff-looking but ornate Louis XIV daybed at the end of the long room, where the boy lay still.

The room was dimly lit, as usual.

"This lighting will not do," the Doctor said to Dimonius.

The man chuckled, clapped his hands. None of the figures stirred. Dimonius shrugged, immediately going from lamp to lamp, turning them to their fullest extent. Two of the figures, a young girl and a youngish man, hissed. Dimonius hissed back menacingly. "Get out if the light offends you!"

The two complainants looked at one another and instead pulled a blood-flecked embroidered quilt over them both.

Dimonius laughed. "Does that meet your needs, Doctor?"

The Doctor nodded. He leant down to the boy, who was clearly in a bad way, placed his special case carefully on the floor and tugged at its steel fasteners.

"How many, tonight?" he asked Dimonius.

The man looked amused, slightly sheepish, shrugged.

"How many tonight, for Joe?" the Doctor said, insistently, feeling in his bag for the correct equipment.

Dimonius shrugged again. "I don't know, I lost count. Eight? Nine?"

The Doctor sighed. Vincent grunted.

"They're in the basement," said Dimonius. "Joe and his men went downstairs after you came in. I know you don't like to see, or to cross paths. You fear it *unlucky*."

"It's nothing to do with luck." The Doctor looked down at the boy, estimated his age to be around twelve, thirteen perhaps. From the look, and smell, of him, he was an urchin. One who would never be missed on London's crowded, careless streets. He took the boy's wrist in his hand and fumbled with his pocket-watch, taking the pulse. "It's weak."

"See!" said Dimonius. "Still alive…"

"He won't be for long," said the Doctor, tersely.

"Are you going to give him a transfusion?" said Vincent.

"Yes, give the boy some *blood*." Dimonius smiled like the Cheshire Cat.

"Yes, I will have to." The Doctor wished, more than anything, that he could take the boy away from here, steal into the night, never come here again. But to what end? What would he do with a poor street-arab? And if he managed to save this one, there were thousands more, dirt-poor, parentless, without a hope, who would do anything for a shilling or a shiny penny even, and the promise of hot chocolate or a rosy cube of Turk's Delight.

He pulled the syringe from his bag and unfurled the two rubber tubes. Then he took a small rosewood box from the bag and selected two long needles, affixing one to the end of each tube. He nodded to Vincent, who obligingly started rolling up his sleeve.

Dimonius was instantly at Vincent's shoulder. "Ah yes, my delicious little blood-bag. What a treasure you are. Your blood is so strong…and so, so tasty!"

Vincent snarled.

The Doctor applied one needle to the crook of Vincent's elbow and the other to the child's arm and began the procedure. Dimonius watched, fascinated, eyes glittering in the muted firelight.

The child did not need much, and they soon saw colour return to his fish-belly cheeks. The Doctor removed the needle from the boy's arm, and from Vincent's, and folded the syringe into a clean white tea-towel, ready for cleaning when they returned to Finsbury.

Dimonius sighed, with pleasure or satisfaction or anticipation, the Doctor could not tell. "So?" he said.

"You'll get another night out of him," said the Doctor. "Feed the boy when he awakes, and he'll be stronger."

Dimonius nodded.

The Doctor pulled the boy's ragged, filthy collar down. Two puncture wounds. He felt a dull, redundant ire rise in him and pulled his eyes away from the sight.

Vincent leaned in to take a look, then pulled Dimonius by his collar, hissed in his ear. "You *idiot*, what have I told you?"

Dimonius made a tight-lipped, guilty smile.

Vincent bared his teeth. "Never the carotid, I said. Did I or did I not say that? Are you even listening to me, you sack of *shit*?"

"Never the carotid," echoed Dimonius, meekly.

"Always take venous blood," said the Doctor. He could hear the defeat in his voice. He closed his eyes, let the nauseating odour of the room flood into his nostrils. He was tired, so, so tired. He struggled to recall his last satisfying sleep but could not. What kind of life was this? "The arm. Much better from the arm."

Dimonius let out a soft wailing sound. His eyes glittered malevolently. "But Doctor, it tastes so much better from the neck!"

Vincent groaned. "Listen, *wampyri* scum. You exist at our pleasure, is that understood? You are a significant drain on public funds and a gigantic pain in the arse to boot. Do you think we enjoy trekking out to this shithole at all hours to clean up your mess? The one thing – the *only* thing – we ask in return, no, insist upon is NO FUCKING NEW ONES!!!" He grabbed Dimonius by the ear, twisting it hard.

Dimonius squealed.

"Do you understand me?" rasped Vincent. "If you take from the artery, you risk turning them!! If I find out you've turned another, it will be Valentine's Day all over again. Do you remember that, glutton? Do you want that? Eh?"

Dimonius shook his head. Vincent released the man and Dimonius slumped into a nearby armchair, whether cowering or sulking it was difficult to ascertain.

Vincent loomed over him, grabbed the arms of the chair, sinking his powerful fingers into the stuffing. "You are *useful*, so we *indulge* you, that's our agreement. But Whitehall does not want a pack of *wampyri* urchins rampaging around the East End. Do you understand me? You are only as useful as I say you are, and if we have to clean house here, we will. You lot are ten-a-penny in the Crimea. I'll just get the Army to hunt me down a different pack to live in the lap of luxury here."

"But Navarino…Hyderabad…*Rorke's Drift*." It was Dimonius' go-to, this list of achievements.

The Doctor sighed, mopped his brow with a handkerchief.

"Oh, fucking RORKE'S DRIFT!!" snapped Vincent. "Rorke's bloody Drift, that's all we hear. Listen, you'd all have been *dog-meat* if the Zulus had not attacked at night. He knelt by the creature, his tone suddenly subdued yet no less menacing for it. "Look, Dimonius, my friend. You have been very useful to us, we know that. We couldn't have managed without you against the Boers and yes, you did help us put down the Manhattan Commune. We are grateful, but you need to play by the rules. Do you *understand*?"

Dimonius nodded.

"Good, then we're understood. Doc, are you ready? I think my camphor is due to wear off, and as you know, the stench of this place has a funny effect on me."

"Yes, of course, let's go," said the Doctor. He remembered very well the last time Vincent had let the miasma of this dreadful place penetrate his defences. The Irishman had turned right there and then and ripped four of the *wampyri* to shreds. The Doctor had been terrified of Vincent since that moment. The Ministry had not been happy, but then its netherworld operatives were prone to step over the bounds from time to time.

Vincent growled and followed the Doctor out onto the landing. They made their way down the stairs, through the hallway and out of the door, remounted the Automatic Cabriolet, and moved swiftly into the night.

As they rolled, the Night Doctor looked out of one window, watching the gas lamps flit by, and Vincent looked out of the other, scouting for breakfast.

ΨΨΨΨΨΨ

ᴛʜᴇ FLOWER GIRLS

Tʜᴇʏ'ᴅ ᴀʟʟ ᴡᴏɴᴅᴇʀᴇᴅ who would pick up Eliza's pitch after the consumption had taken her this winter past. It was a terrible thing, to be sure, but the flower girls worked outside in all weathers and most considered it only a matter of time before some blight or other would do for them too.

Fannie – the oldest of the group, unless you counted Esther, which nobody really did – wished she could have afforded it. She'd have sub-let it and there would have been plenty of takers, for Covent Garden Market pitches were the best in the city. But Fannie was short of coin. These days business went to the younger, prettier girls, especially those with a more creative eye, and while Fannie's bouquets were up to the job, she was not one to get giddy over the latest trends, nor fuss with the Frenchified wraps demanded by the sophisticated ladies or the gentlemen aiming to court them.

C'mon Fannie Douglas, you may be forty, but you've still got most of your teeth and these girls still look up to you, even if you ain't quite as fancy as some of them.

"Look there, that must be her!"

Fannie followed Clarrie's pointing finger to Mr Bleecker and the young, pretty thing beside him.

"Ooh, I wonder what she'll be like?" Lorna and Clarrie, the youngest of the group, seemed eager to make a new friend.

Fannie brushed snippets of cut stem off her apron. *She* would be first to greet the newcomer and to teach her what she needed to know. The new girl's pitch was right next to hers, after all. That was plenty reason, right there.

She was a treat to look at, this one, skin like alabaster and a pointy chin that all the gents craved after that Conan Doyle had got them all genned up with his talk of faeries. She'd be a Scot for sure, what with those green eyes and tumble of red hair. Or Irish maybe. What was the difference? On the London streets, they were all paupers, the Celts. Still, this girl wasn't destitute. Her maroon shawl looked new, machine-made, and her cream blouse was surely a gent's gift, teamed perfectly with a plain skirt and well-turned bootees.

The pitch manager flashed a tight smile at Fannie as they arrived. "This here is Lorelei. She'll be taking over Eliza's pitch." He turned to the red-haired girl. "This is it. Your weekly rent includes this rack, your daily box below and a frigorific cask to store your blooms overnight. Fannie here will show you the ropes."

The girl nodded and smiled at Fannie.

Fannie clipped the stem of a carnation which had seen better days. "Lorelei, aw that's such a pretty name for such a pretty flower."

The girl blushed.

"You are, dear!" She put the wilting carnation down, took Lorelei's arm, and nodded to Mr Bleecker. He left, seemingly satisfied.

"Your rack is right next to mine," said Fannie, "so I'll be able to keep an eye on you and mind your things when you need to spend a penny. We'll be fast friends, I'm sure."

With the manager gone, the other girls gathered around.

"I'm Clarrie, this is Lottie, Esther, Pauline, Lorna…" Clarrie excitedly flung name after name at Lorelei, who nodded to each of them in turn.

"Come on now, Clarrie!" Fannie waved a hand at the dark-haired waif. "You'll confuse the poor girl! There'll be time soon enough for gabbing and finding out what you all want to know. Shoo now, you silly geese. We'll take Lorelei down to the Landing soon, show her how things are done in the Market."

The girls nodded to Lorelei and went back to their racks, exchanging whispers and giggling as they did so.

Fannie turned to Lorelei and brought her hand up to the girl's cheek. "A rare bloom, I do declare."

Lorelei smiled, flushed red and shrank gently away from Fannie's hand.

Fannie was unperturbed. Cultivation took time. "No need to be ashamed of it. You'll do very well in the Market, trust me. When the beaus and dandies get a look at you, your carnations and roses will be gone, quick as a flash!" She took a solitary red rose from the few flowers left on her rack and held it out for her new charge. "Roses, you want to be a bit careful with. They're expensive, and it's only gentlemen who will plump for a nice rose, so mind how many you have on your rack. And always put them up high, so's they can be seen. Two colours, always. White is steady but I find it a bit funereal. Yellow's a good bet, if you can get them, though there's been some wretched Colombian bug feasting on the yellows, my man was telling me. Red, like this, you should always have but only ever a dozen, if you can afford it. A dozen's the most a gentleman will ever buy, and then only if it's a big love, and that's a big day for you too! But mostly you'll sell singles and even then, not that many. Depends on how drunk the scoundrels get, 'cause if they're not sozzled they'll only ever buy a single for their floozy."

Fannie stopped herself abruptly. "Ah well, perhaps you knows all this already, my chuckaboo, eh?"

Lorelei "Oh, no, no. It was very helpful, truly."

"Is this the first time you've had a pitch?"

"I used to help out, down at the Vauxhall Reaches, but this is the first pitch of my own."

Vauxhall Reaches? Fannie wondered how long ago that was. The girl couldn't be more than seventeen or eighteen, surely, and the Reaches had closed down when Vauxhall had been gentrified a few years back. "Well, that's lovely then, I'll teach you what I know. As my old ma used to say: 'learn once and forget it, learn twice and get it'. I was talking to you of gentlemen. Ladies will buy flowers too of course, but they'll be tending to buy single blooms, sometimes a few so's they can make up their own posy."

"Oh?"

"Oh yes! For when they have a gentleman courting them, they'll often want to send the fellow a signal, do you understand?"

"A signal?"

Fannie moved closer, put her right hand to the left side of her mouth. "Yes. They call it the Language of Flowers, so they do. The bud of a white rose, that means a heart that is ignorant of love. A striped carnation is for refusal of an advance, while the Lady's Slipper means 'win me and wear me'." She laughed then, a lusty growl which caused the others to look over at the pair of them.

"Don't be giving the girl *all* your secrets!" Esther waved her finger at Fannie and grinned at Lorelei. "She'll learn soon enough."

Fannie put her arm around Lorelei. "Well, I'm not gonna let any of those buggers at the Landing hoodwink my pretty little Lorelei, I can tell you that. If any of them try to fleece her or pass off any old rubbish on her, they're gonna have to answer to Fannie Douglas!" She shook one hefty-looking, reddened fist in the air. Nearly thirty years selling flowers in all weathers, dipping her hands into buckets of cold water and trimming stems with her trusty pocket-knife meant Fannie's hands were more like those of a prizefighter than a lady, and she flattered herself she knew how to use them.

The girls set off for the walk to the Landing. Clarrie and Lorna bowed deeply to one another then each took the other's arm, a little game they liked to play. A couple of the other girls laughed and began a faux wedding dance, casting imaginary rose petals before the happy couple. Esther acted as maid of honour, taking up the invisible train behind Clarrie and humming the Wedding March.

Beneath them came a low rumble and a deep groan as if the earth was rearranging itself below. The square seemed to shudder, the flower racks wobbled slightly, panes of glass rattled in the casements of nearby shops.

Lorelei looked about nervously.

Fannie squeezed her closer. "It's just the pneumatic railway, dearie, goes right under here. The Piccadilly and Brompton Line rides closer to the surface than any other line, I'm given to understand, that's why we can hear it. One of the engineers told me there's a crick in the track, right here, so some trains make an awful racket going over them."

The last of the train noise faded, and as if to get Fannie back for her mistrust, a jet of foul-smelling steam shot from a pavement grate just in front of the wedding party. The girls screamed with laughter and ran pell-mell down towards the Strand, waving their hands over their noses.

Fannie looked at the grate. "Well, that's a fine thing, isn't it? That crick in the track will make for a fine pickle, someday, you mark my words. I don't doubt those automatic trains are a marvellous invention, but you wouldn't get me on one of them for love nor money."

Fannie and Lorelei soon caught up with Esther who had fallen behind on account of her age and her gammy leg, so the three of them walked slowly down to the Strand behind a grocer's lad slow-walking a cart of apples and other penny-fruit. Lorelei walked with her head down, chewing the side of her lip.

"What is it, my chuckaboo?" asked Fannie.

Lorelei managed a half smile, but her face was pale, frown lines carving gentle wrinkles into her porcelain brow. "Oh, oh, it's nothing, first day nerves I suppose."

"Ah, well, that's only to be expected, dearie."

The Strand was busy with costermongers' carts, Hansom cabs and all manner of foot traffic. The grocer's lad let them have three bruised apples for a farthing each, and they strolled contentedly, munching their breakfast.

"Crunchy apples and a crisp Spring morn," said Esther. "What could be better?"

Fannie clasped Lorelei's arm. "There, you see, my lovely. What could be better?"

Presently, they caught up to the other girls, who had stopped to gawk at something of a commotion by the junction of the Strand and the Aldwych.

A large four-wheeled vehicle lay tilted by the side of the road next to Somerset House, one of its huge, notched wheels apparently caught in a drain. It was a beast of a machine, with a bulbous boiler and long, curved stack up front, carrying four cylindrical silos. The boiler was leaking steam from various joints, and several men were trying to repair it.

"It looks like an upside-down olyphant!" shrieked Clarrie.

"Where have you been seeing olyphants?" Fannie raised a sceptical eyebrow.

Clarrie planted her hands on her hips. "At the Regent's Park Zoo!"

"When have you had time or coin for the Zoo?" scoffed Fannie.

Lorna piped up. "'er gentleman took 'er."

"Who's this gentleman, Clarrie?" said Fannie.

"Oh, he's awful fancy," giggled Lorna.

Clarrie held up one finger to her mouth. "Shhhh! He don't like nobody knowing. But he's very kind to me. Bought me a lovely garter and when we went to the Zoo I had Italian ice! It's lovely…" She slipped into happy reverie as they walked. "He always makes me wear a posy when we go out. He chooses the blooms very carefully, and he's very particular about where I wears it."

Lorna cackled and elbowed one of the other girls. "I bet he is!"

"I'm gonna keep a sharp eye out for him," said Fannie. "Maybe he'll have an older gentleman friend he can introduce to me."

There was laughter, though none of it cruel. Everyone knew Fannie hadn't grabbed any gentleman's attention for years, though in fairness now she was barren she could make some easy extra coin at the Docks, if the fancy took her.

"It's called a Ruston engine," said Lorelei, quietly. "That one produces six nhp, er, nominal horse power. That's how many horses it would take to give the same pull."

Fannie looked at her in astonishment. "How do you know that? Perhaps you've a fancy gent yourself, taught you that?"

Lorelei tipped her head on one side so that she might examine the engine in its adjusted plane. "My father was an engineer."

The girls nodded approvingly, for the most part, though none had the slightest interest in mechanical things, then picked up their route again.

Lorelei lingered, seemingly fascinated by the huge engine.

There's more to this one than meets the eye. Fannie took up her younger charge's arm again and pulled her gently away from the sight. As she did so, she was convinced they were being watched. Sure enough, as they passed by Somerset House, Fannie noticed a figure in the shade of the pillars at the front entryway, a big fellow with a wrestler's build, in a brown bowler or possibly a derby with a half-frock coat and pants which finished a little above his calf-boots, as was the mode. The man was looking directly at them. As he saw them looking towards him, he drew a cheroot from his pocket and made to light it with his left hand.

A southpaw, eh? I might have known.

"What's wrong?" asked Lorelei.

Fannie's expression grew dark. "That place gives me the creeps. There's always someone watching you from the gate. And that one looks like a real skilamalink."

"What is it, that place?"

"Government records, they say, though one of the market-runners told me it's where the Dark Lanterns hang…" Fannie peered into the shadows to get a better look, but the man had disappeared.

"Dark Lanterns?"

"Shhhh!!"

"Dark Lanterns?" This time Lorelei spoke quietly.

Fannie did the same. "It's all new, that, according to a gentleman acquaintance of mine who's pretty free with his words after a glass of absinthe. They've no uniforms, it seems, nor helmets. A kind of secretive police, I suppose. They're not based at Scotland Yard, but there, behind all that marble and pillars and what-not, so they say."

"They say? Who are 'they'?"

Fannie struggled to read the girl's expression. The beautiful porcelain face was the picture of calm, but a few tiny cracks had appeared at the edges of Lorelei's eyes and mouths. Worry-lines, her old ma would have called them. "Oh, you know, scuttlebutt, street-talk, nothing more. Still, nothing we need fear, eh? Us simple flower sellers keep ourselves to ourselves and don't bring nothing but joy to the world."

Lorelei nodded and smiled. "I'm sure you're right."

The Temple Landing was a mass of colour this morning. The Flower Men had fully six varieties of tulips from the Spanish Netherlands and Flanders, pretty as you like. There were roses from under the Sussex Glass, the bluest Spring gentian from Durham, daffodils from Gloucestershire – there were masses of them at this time of year, so the daffs were cheap as a tinker's Christmas. Then there were carnations, irises and lilies which had become year-round staples thanks to the famed Hague Glass, which Fannie dreamed of seeing one day.

"Now, if you need me to help you…" started Fannie.

"No, no, that's fine," said Lorelei, brightly. "Your advice earlier was very helpful. I'll stick with that."

The younger girl went through the vendors like an expert, picking the finest blooms, rejecting what many sought to offload onto the apparent ingenue, negotiating keen prices with the most winsome smile and finally coming away with a very interesting crop, including some seasonal favourites, of course, and plenty of greenery.

She's done this before, thought Fannie. *But she never said anything, just let me witter on like a prize plum.*

Fannie's purse was a little parched, so she stuck to solid sellers like violet and primroses as well as a few of the daffs, though she wouldn't make much profit on them. She did have one nice find, bog-rosemary all the way from Kirkcudbright. Such delicate pink flowers would probably not sell off the rack, but she fancied she could shift them to one or two of the lady florists up

Neal Street, who were too grand to come down to the Landing but who liked to gussy up their bouquets with more unusual blooms just to fox their snooty Bloomsbury customers.

You've still got it, Fannie Douglas. There's life in the old dog yet.

ΨΨΨΨΨΨ

Fannie continued to observe Lorelei over the next two weeks. As the days rolled on, the memory of her gabbled advice when they'd first met embarrassed Fannie to the point of going whole days saying barely a word to her would-be protégée, but the girl treated her with nothing but kindness, which made matters worse.

Lorelei was a talented florist, for sure, no ingenue. While the other girls fiddled around making tussie-mussies and nosegays which sold for a penny, tuppence or even threepence if they had something about them, Lorelei crafted more confident, expensive bouquets.

Eventually, Fannie plucked up the courage to break out of her near silence. "Well, my chuckaboo, seems you're a natural!"

The girl beamed at her, a smile of such warmth and tenderness that Fannie blushed to her roots, and they fell into being fast friends once again.

There was one oddity, something which nagged at Fannie though she couldn't put her finger on why. With notable frequency, working men, clad in their Sunday best – always with a flat cap, never a gent's hat – would make a beeline for Lorelei's stall, passing by all the other girls. To a man, they'd buy a single stem, always a yellow flower, buttonhole it, and go about their business.

What kind of man buys a single yellow rose? Never mind a single yellow carnation!

On one occasion, two of the men came to Lorelei. They stood for a minute, seemingly arguing, but Fannie was serving a customer and could not make out anything they were saying. One of the men then persuaded the other to purchase a flower, a yellow rose again, and they left.

Scattered amid the more regular, browsing customers who were attracted by Lorelei's lovely bouquets and her winning, winsome smile, the men would not have garnered much attention. But in her thirty years and more behind the racks Fannie knew the quality of traffic, and this regularity of common men did not sit well with her, not here.

On their regular visits to the Landing to restock, Fannie tried to wheedle more information from the engineer's daughter, but the girl had such a charm about her, was so clever, she'd always have a way of turning the conversation back to Fannie, gulling the older woman into revealing quite intimate details of her life without divulging any similar stories.

After a few days of this, Fannie decided to give up her enquiries, not because she wasn't interested, but because Lorelei clearly wanted to keep herself to herself. And while she was scant with her information, the girl was more than generous otherwise to her friend. She'd often come through with a tasty morsel for lunch, lend Fannie a penny here or there when she was boracic, and once brought some homemade jam for all the girls

Esther was not convinced. "I can tell machine-made jam a mile away!"

"Oh, shush," said Fannie. "Stop your nonsense. It's a lovely gesture, even if she did buy it on the Portobello Market."

"Hmmph."

Early one rainy Wednesday, they made their way down to the Landing for the midweek restock.

Right down by the end of the Landing next to the privies was an unfamiliar vendor, a dark-coated man with a sallow expression and a Turkish moustache. Fannie was a creature of habit, and always fought shy of new vendors, especially those with a rum look about them, but Lorelei made straight for the man. Fannie was minded to say something, but as she paid over two shillings Lorelei had lent her in exchange for a fulsome bunch of red-striped carnations, thought better of it.

Fannie caught up with the girl on the way back and cast her experienced eye over what she was forced to admit was an impressive selection, marred only by the inclusion of some very run-of-the-mill country blooms. "Aw, that's a fine collection and no mistake, even those pretty yellows."

"Yes, kingcups I think they're called."

"I know what they are, my love. I've seen every flower that's ever growed, in my time. But they're rare, here."

"Oh," said Lorelei. "They seem fairly ordinary to me."

"That they are!" Fannie laughed, though she was puzzled as to why the girl had bought them if she thought they were 'ordinary'. "No, I didn't mean rare like that, I meant rare as in we don't see them much round here.

They're a flower from up country a ways, where my old auntie used to live in King's Lynn. We'd pick them from roadside ditches or around ponds when I was a girl."

"Ah. Well, I thought they were pretty."

"Yes, that they are. That they are."

What, Fannie wondered, were all those kingcups going to be used for?

Nothing, it seemed. Lorelei tucked them away in her daily box, under her rack.

Now there's a mystery and no mistake. What – or who – are you saving them for?

By mid-afternoon, Lorelei had sold most of her stock and was turning customers away, sending them to the other girls.

Why don't you sell those kingcups if you've run out of stock, my chuckaboo?

ΨΨΨΨΨΨ

The bells of St Clement Danes pealed forth the three o'clock, English Proper Time.

Fannie was tired, though not from activity. The striped carnations she'd invested most of her money in had not shifted, for some reason she couldn't divine. She sat, disconsolately, on the step behind her rack, finishing up a morsel of German pumpernickel she'd bought for her lunch, when a tall gentleman appeared at Lorelei's pitch.

Fannie regarded him curiously. He wouldn't stand out in the modish West End crowd, with a green velvet top hat wound with burgundy cord, and a gaberdine coat with a neat fur collar, such as she had seen in pictures from the Crimea, but there was something distinctly *off* about him. Perhaps it was his spectacles, the copper frame so light it seemed only to be made from wire, and the lenses dark, as an albino might wear, though the man had brown hair and tanned skin, so was altogether not an albino. Or maybe it was the way he held himself, tight, like a coiled spring, as if he meant to bolt at any second.

The man took two shillings from his waistcoat pocket and dropped them into Lorelei's outstretched hand.

She's got no flowers left! What are you buying with those two shillings?

From under her rack, Lorelei drew out six of the king-cups and laid them beside three orange-mouthed jonquils and a single sprig of daphne, wrapped in green silk-paper with fine yellow string. She handed them to the man.

He looked at the wrapped flowers, then looked at Lorelei. Was it Fannie's imagination, or did something unspoken pass between them?

The man turned on his heel without so much as a 'goodbye' or a 'thank you' and disappeared into the milling crowd.

Two shillings! For a sixer of marsh marigolds? They grow like a plague in the Cambridge fens! No wonder the girl was able to be so generous.

Fannie felt the first few spots of rain, and soon, the crowd in the Market had quite disappeared, off to take a late afternoon chocolate in one of the fancy Belgian cafes or heading home for their tea.

"That's it for the day I suppose." Fannie packed up her rack and her remaining flowers and went to put them in her padlocked cool box, which sat at the end of a row of identical boxes all the girls rented, under the far gallery. The blooms would go another few days in the special cool boxes, an invention of Lord Daire, who had developed his Frigorific Cask in the Tropics and become a millionaire upon his return to Britain.

"I'm going to find a gin and some nice salt beef on Cheapside before I go back to my lodgings…" she began, looking around for Lorelei, but the girl was gone.

ΨΨΨΨΨΨ

The next morning, Fannie was itching to find out more about Lorelei's mystery customer and determined to ask her on the way down to the Landing, where the girl would doubtless head to restock after selling virtually all her flowers the day before.

But her plan was defeated. The Landing was closed for the arrival of the newest steam clipper to grace the Thames. Lorelei instead gave her time generously to the other girls, showing them how to tie bouquets with fancy French knots, and sharing some of the beautiful wrappings and ribbons she'd brought with her in a carpet bag.

The bag was new. Fannie fancied the girl must have brought it with her from her previous pitch, wherever that was. Somewhere well to do, obviously, perhaps Kensington or Notting Hill Gate.

Helping out at Vauxhall Reaches my knobbly behind!

The day brightened as it went along, though Fannie had no more luck shifting her striped carnations than she had the day before. She begged a little bread and cheese off Esther, promised to get her back when she could, but as morning wore into afternoon, her stomach was growling. She couldn't help but wonder where her next meal might be coming from.

Then, once again at the three o'clock, the gentleman in the green topper came to Lorelei's position.

He drew two shillings from his pocket without even counting them out and passed them to Lorelei. Then he said: "The six blooms yesterday were most satisfactory. I hope you will thank your vendor for me. I daresay they will last until the mistress of the house returns."

Lorelei nodded. "Very good sir, I will pass along your thanks. I have heard that my vendor is very keen on *nasturtiums*."

"As are we all."

"Should I obtain some for you?"

Green Topper seemed to think. "Not for now, thank you. Perhaps next week. Let's see what comes of these kingcups, shall we?" He turned, doffed his hat to Lorelei and left.

Fannie was amazed. *Another two shillings, for nothing?* She decided to keep her counsel. Surely this was nothing but a gent taking a fancy to a pretty girl. Besides, she was too tired and too hungry to make anything of it.

"Are you ok, Fannie?"

"Aw, yes my dear, of course I'm fine. You have some generous customers."

"I'm very fortunate." Lorelei smiled warmly.

There was nothing more to be said about it, and Fannie busied herself with her end of day doings.

Still, the question nagged at her. She had to find out more. "Will you come with me to the White Hart at the bottom of Chancery Lane this evening, dear? I thought we might get a gin to warm our hearts."

The White Hart was a very reputable establishment and usually out of Fannie's price range, though she was sure Lorelei could afford it and more. Fannie would surely be able to get something out of the girl, in the warm, with a little gin to loosen their tongues.

"Oh, Fannie, it's a lovely offer but I'm tired. Perhaps another night. I'd better get back to St Pancras. My rent is due, and I don't like to be late with it." She pressed two shillings into Fannie's hand. "I've had a very lucky couple of days and am so thankful to you for your friendship. Here, take this. I've heard they roast their hams in honey and cloves at the White Hart. Get some for your dinner, my treat."

Fannie was stumped. The girl had been generous before – a hot chocolate here, a little sausage there – but nothing on this scale.

She stared at the coins as if they were magic. She mumbled a thank you, but Lorelei had already turned away and was walking quickly across the paved square towards Leicester Square for her omnibus, waving and smiling as she went.

Fannie shrugged. Her stomach was grumbling, and her mouth began to water at the thought of the honeyed ham, so she made for the White Hart.

I've been bought for a shilling before, but never for two.

ΨΨΨΨΨΨ

The two shillings went much further than she thought, and Fannie finished the night at the Drowned Rat in

Wapping, singing at the top of her lungs while the steam pianola ran the gamut of musical hall favourites.

The next morning, she had the hangover of death.

"Read all about it! Read all about it!" The raucous paperboy could be heard the length and breadth of Covent Garden.

"I do wish he'd read and not shout!" Fannie rubbed her head.

"One too many gins last night, eh?" Esther cackled and nudged Lorna who tittered like a baby bird. "New month, new resolution. Maybe not drink til May, eh?"

"I blame the Drowned Rat and their ferocious brass-brewed ale!" said Fannie. "What is that paperboy going on about now?"

"Six banks raided in six hours! Doors blown clean off! Rad plot suspected! Police warn of bombing campaign!"

Fannie was shocked. "Is that an April Fool?"

"No!" Esther flapped at her face. "It's true! I heard it off a gent last night, so I did, but I thought he was having me on! The Rads, again! What will become of us?"

"You think the Rads are going to bomb a bunch of flower girls, do you, Esther?" Fannie rolled her eyes, but she was aware her voice was quavering. "Your head must be full of cloth."

Lorelei appeared at the rack next to her. "What's all the commotion?"

Fannie smiled as much as her hangover would allow. "Oh, the Rads getting uppity, so it seems." She belched, then shivered as a wave of nausea washed over her.

"Oh." If the girl was worried about the Rad activity, she gave no sign. "I was thinking to get a lemon tea on the way down to the Landing, will you join me?"

Fannie groaned. "I don't know that I have the strength, my chuckaboo. I have a touch of the vapours I think."

"Vapours!" Esther scoffed.

Lorelei pointedly ignored the older woman. "Lemon tea is just the thing for the vapours, trust me. Two cubes of clove sugar in it and you'll be right as rain."

Fannie attempted a smile and staggered to her feet.

Lorelei took her by the arm, and they made their slow way to the Temple Landing, taking a lemon tea and clove sugars from the Italian vendor at the bottom of Burleigh Street. When they reached the Landing, the girl went directly to the Turk, while Fannie wandered blearily at the cheap end by the waste barge, where she managed to find a few hyacinths which would go a day or two and some pansies from one of the older vendors there who'd taken a shine to her.

Conversation was in short supply on the way back to the Market. Fannie tried to get a look at what Lorelei had had off the Turk, but the blooms were wrapped up against the first showers of April. Fannie resolved to take a peek while Lorelei was preparing, but by the time they'd made the gentle climb to the Market, her stomach was feeling very queer and she had to make a stop to vomit down a drain. Flowers were the last thing on her mind.

Lunchtime came and went, with Fannie refusing all but a couple of swigs of small beer from Esther's brown bottle.

Green Topper arrived on the strike of three.

Fannie made a show of serving a customer while watching out of the corner of her eye. Exactly as before, Green

Topper took coins from his pocket and placed them in Lorelei's hand.

Another two shillings. What will he get for his coin this time?

"Thank you, sir." Lorelei bent under the rack to her daily storage box and retrieved a bouquet.

Fannie looked over at the flowers. They were out of season, from under the Hague Glass or maybe the Sussex, come to that. There was a stem of a bushy purple flower she recognised. *Gravel root is it?* With it was a single large, grey-green iris and one large daisy, all backed with eight slim ferns. *Most peculiar, especially that ugly iris. Whoever this gentleman is trying to impress must be an odd bird and no mistake!*

Fannie glanced at the man as he left but fancied he saw her, so she cast her eyes in the other direction entirely to put him off. Right in her eyeline was a man, stood under the arches next to the eastern entrance to the Market, his brown derby hat clearly visible in the light of the dipping sun. Fannie struggled to recall where she had seen him before. He took out a cheroot and lit it with his left hand, and then she knew.

Dark Lantern.

"Are you recovered, Fannie?" Lorelei touched her arm.

Fannie started. "Oh, my dear, I fairly jumped out of my skin then!" She turned to Lorelei, then turned back to remark on Brown Derby, but the man had gone.

"Oh, I'm sorry. What's the matter?"

"Nothing, dearie, I'm quite fine." Fannie decided to take her chance. "That was an unusual bouquet your gentleman had."

"Yes, yes it was. He has very specific tastes. He's been a customer of mine for a few years now. Followed me here from Vauxhall Reaches."

"Did he now? That was your last pitch, wasn't it?"

"Yes, that's right. Nice and close to the Flower Market by Nine Elms."

"Yes, dear, I daresay it was."

A week or so back you were just helping at the Reaches, now you had your own pitch there? Fannie's stomach quivered, whether a last gasp of the hangover or something else she could not tell. She racked her brains to try to remember when the developments went in, when the flower sellers by the Reaches had dispersed to Victoria, Trafalgar Square, here in the Market.

Something here doesn't make sense.

"Fannie?" Lorelei was tugging at her arm.

"Yes?"

"Are you sure you're alright?"

"I'm fine dear, right as ninepence."

Lorelei smiled and turned away to begin packing up.

Fannie did not pursue Lorelei that evening. She was tired and hungry, and any intrigue was just as likely to be in her own head than real.

Still, the identity of the strange iris ate at her. She prided herself on her knowledge of flowers and on her memory, but both came up blank.

Nothing for it, Fannie you old mare, but to consult the Marchioness!

Fannie had picked up the well-worn copy of *The Language of Flowers*, by Lady Elspeth McGovern-Smythe, Marchioness of Steeltown Rashes, from a bookseller by

St James's Park. She wasn't much of a reader, having had little in the way of education, but she liked a good picture, and the book was not only full of handsome inked illustrations but had a set of glossy plates at its centre. She'd often flicked through it, reading aloud as her finger traced the words, trying to remember them so she could impress the girls.

She lit her reading candle, took the book from its shelf, wrapped her good shawl about her and settled herself in her single battered armchair, with a small chunk of fruit-cake she'd had from her landlady to accompany her tea as she read.

"Gravel root, ha!" She had been right about the purple bush. "Also known as Sweet Joe-Pye-Weed. How the devil did you forget a thing like that, Fannie Douglas?" Her eye strayed past the botanical notes to a single word in block capitals, relating what the flower would mean to a gent if he spied his *amoureuse* wearing or carrying it.

DELAY.

She laughed, spitting a little tea onto her shawl. "Imagine him seeing that on 'er! He'd be away to his lodgings to take care of himself, that night." She wiped the errant splash of tea from her and hunted for the iris. "G…H…I…here we are! Irises. I knew I'd seen you before, you ugly thing! It was that doctor back at the Hyde Park racks, claimed e'd come from "ze" Palace if you please! Spoke like a German and looked like one too, with his bushy moustache, bushy beard and bushy eyebrows.

And there it was, plain as day. German Iris or *Bearded* Iris! Wasn't that funny. German *and* with a beard. Again, her eye was drawn by the single word denoting the flower's alleged meaning.

FLAME or FIRE.

"What a dull bloom to be taking about fire! My, my, delay and fire. What's that about?"

She decided to look up the other flowers, but broke off a piece of fruitcake first, to help finish her tea.

"Detectiving is hungry work!"

Listen to you, Fannie Douglas, talking to yourself like a mad old woman.

She flicked back to the 'D' section where Daisies (various) were to be found.

It was a handsome one, Lorelei's, but didn't seem especially distinctive. That was annoying, there were eight or nine different types, and each had a separate meaning.

How's a gent supposed to figure all this? You're having trouble and you've had thirty years behind the racks!

Could be anything. Might even be something very ordinary. She ran her finger down the list of meanings. I SHARE YOUR SENTIMENTS. FAREWELL. BEAUTY. INNOCENCE.

A dab of fruitcake passed from her finger to the page. "Look now, Fannie, you'll ruin this!" But her eye was drawn to the reference, in smaller print, clearly less consequential to her ladyship. "Also known as the flower symbolic of APRIL."

That seemed to fit with DELAY. Delay until something, surely. Could be 'farewell', she supposed. A delayed farewell? But then, either way, what was the FIRE about?

What else? Oh, the fern stalks. *Eight* fern stalks.

"F…F…where are you?"

Fern. Didn't seem quite right, greenery having its own signals, surely, but there it was: FASCINATION. She shook her head.

DELAY. FIRE. FAREWELL. FASCINATION.

This was surely nonsense. "You're a silly goose, Fannie Douglas. This can't be nothing but nonsense. They said your imagination runs away with you, and so it has! Right down to the river and jumped in!"

But it nagged at her. The bouquets Lorelei made for Green Topper were so specific, so strange, especially given the artistry and attention to colour and balance in all the others she sold.

Fannie picked on the most troubling of the definitions, the fern. *That doesn't seem right, eight fascinations.* She'd used ferns plenty of times, but had never used eight of the things, it was far too much for a single bouquet. Eight? Was that it? Number eight?

"Come on Fannie, put it all together and what do you have?" The Marchioness was a grand master when it came to the meaning of individual flowers but had ignored bouquets entirely. Maybe Fannie should write a book...

EIGHT. FIRE. APRIL. DELAY.

That doesn't mean anything, Fannie.

EIGHT. APRIL.

The 8th of April? That might be something.

DELAY.

Delay something until April 8th? That was only a week away. Delay what? Delay the fire? *What fire?*

Absently, she tossed another hefty piece of old planking into the fireplace. She'd been drying the planks all winter as they made good, quick heat when she couldn't afford coal. She stared into it, as if the meaning might become clear, but nothing did.

What fire?

She took a sip of tea but felt sick, wondering if it was the fruitcake.

ΨΨΨΨΨΨ

By the time she reached the Market the next day, her belly was complaining as if her throat had been cut. Her efforts of the night before were still jumbling around in her head. She had to ask Lorelei about them.

Lorelei was not by her rack when Fannie arrived, but appeared moments later with two paper cups of hot chocolate, emblazoned with the distinctive blue stamp of the Belgian place on Drury Lane, a café Fannie had always hankered after sampling but had been put off by how fancy it was.

Fannie's mouth watered. "What's this in aid of, my chuckaboo?"

Lorelei smiled. "It's a chilly morning, I thought you might like some. I heard you mention that place."

A tear formed at the corner of Fannie's eye. She wiped it away instantly, pretending the steam had got to her, and gulped greedily at the thick, delicious chocolate.

It was another thin day, and the chocolate only stayed her hunger for a couple of hours. She gave Esther a penny for a chunk of carraway bread and a piece of cheese at lunch, then saw Lorelei watching her as she did. The girl immediately looked away, and Fannie hung her head.

Lorelei came to her late in the afternoon. As usual,

she'd had a good day, though the green-toppered gentleman had not made an appearance. She took up Fannie's hand and pressed three coins into it.

Fannie was aghast. "Oh, dearie, you can't."

"I know three shillings isn't much, but you need to eat, and this will get you something."

"I can't, I can't take charity from you, you just a girl and me a silly old woman who should know better." This time, the tears came in earnest.

Lorelei sat down beside her and put her arm around the older woman.

Fannie could feel the soft, machine-spun wool of the girl's shawl, warm and fresh under her face. "I'm all cried out, so I am." She brought her head up, saw Esther and Clarrie look away, and scowled.

"They're just worried about you," explained Lorelei. "Take the three shillings and treat yourself to something proper. Trust me, your luck will turn, you've just had a bad run."

Fannie wiped her nose with her sleeve and set about packing up. "Right enough. Thank you kindly. I'll get you back for this, don't you worry. I'll show you Fannie Douglas can be the best friend you've ever had."

Lorelei smiled at her.

That evening, Fannie decided to go to the White Hart again, resolved to accept Lorelei's generosity for what it was. Besides, her belly needed something, and the thought of the honeyed ham or even the potted partridge at the Hart was enough of a draw for anyone.

The Hart 'really took the egg', as her old ma would have said. A velveted, warm and smoky establishment full of barristers' clerks from the Temple, the odd frockcoat himself and a few shopkeepers, the Hart had been there since the Great Fire, it was said.

She took a table by one of the grimy windows and was about to order a drink when a somewhat elderly man, a tobacconist by the smell of him, took a fancy to her from his barstool. She beckoned him over and allowed him to buy her a reduced Porto, which arrived in a beautiful crystal goblet which she thought about stealing but decided not to in case she was seen and barred from the place or, worse, turned over to the Peelers. He then proceeded to bore her with tales of leaf, pipe and the correct way to pack a bowl. She was well-used to indulging menfolk and listened politely, nodding here and there and risking the odd "oh, how interesting" or "ooh, that sounds intriguing", despite having no care or interest in their conversation, and this cove was an easy mark in that regard.

Her ear was, however, caught by the dialogue between two clerks at the corner table behind them. They spoke in slightly hushed tones, clearly thinking they could not be overheard in the din of the tavern, but Fannie had sharp hearing, always had done, and she listened intently when her attention was caught by a single word.

"Floriography," said one of the men.

His somewhat hifalutin delivery disguised an Estuary accent, likely out by Southend. Clerks often did that, especially if their barristers were of note. Fannie would call him Prancer, for his airs and graces.

"Florrie-what?" said the second. His was a thick East London accent.

Fannie imagined him cruising the dancehalls of Hackney and Bethnal Green, working his wiles on impressionable dolly-mops. Dancer, then, this one.

"Floriography," said Prancer. "The language of flowers. I been readin' about it."

"A *language*?" said Dancer, clearly somewhat sceptical.

"Yeah, for secret communications."

"What, like in the Navy? 'Ang a bunch of primroses over the side of a battleship and that means port broadside or summing?"

"Nah, ya daft plum, communicating wiv a gent, if you're a lady, like." Prancer finished his pint noisily, called for another.

"I never seen that before," said Dancer.

"Not surprised, the tarts you 'ang around wiv wouldn't know a proper flower from a roadside weed."

"Oi, they're classy girls! They knows about flowers." Dancer pronounced the word flowers *flaars*.

"Anyway, I been reading about it since my man's latest case, you know."

"'Is latest case is about flaars, is it, your Sir Arnold?" said Dancer.

"Well, it's more about how they reckon they might be used in…" his voice dropped, "other ways…you know?"

"What other ways?"

"I dunno, truth be told," said Prancer. "You know Sir Arnold and his bleedin' Dark Lanterns and the Rads they're chasing…"

"Aw all that again…secrets n stuff."

"Yeah, can't talk about it."

"You just did!" Dancer laughed uproariously. "Anyway, you goin' down the track tomorrow?"

"Maybe…"

Their conversation drifted into talk of dogs.

Dark Lanterns! Rads! What if…?

"What say you then, my dear?"

Fannie's attention whipped back to the elderly tobacconist.

The man looked hopeful, sort of sad.

"Oh, I, er…sorry dearie, I drifted away just then, what was it you said?"

The elderly man smiled. "I know I'm not much to look at, so I'm not surprised you're not keen. But we could pick up a bottle of champagne and some bread and sausage at a little place I know just by St Paul's, and was it Whitechapel you said you lodged? I'll pay for a Hansom to there…"

Fannie smiled and sighed. Champagne and sausage and a Hansom home was a fair price for what the man wanted, and he seemed nice enough. "Alright, dearie, I'll get us a little bit of brandy from the bar. Champagne and brandy is nice together." She felt in her pocket for the three shillings, bringing one out for the bottle of gut-rot.

The man nodded, grinned.

'Christmas come in April', as her old ma would say. For both of them, it seemed.

ΨΨΨΨΨΨ

The tobacconist had offered to pay for a cab for Fannie in the morning, even an automatic if she'd have wanted it, but she refused. She'd taken him for enough coin that night, though given good value if she'd say so herself, but fair was fair and he'd been fair enough, so she took the steam omnibus.

She thumbed the Marchioness's dog-eared volume as the omnibus trundled its way down Eastcheap, its brass-faced driver clicking and clacking. She often liked to take the book with her, flick through the pretty illustrations, especially if it was a day for the Landing. She'd slid a piece of matchbox cover between the 'H' and 'I' sections to see if she could figure out anything more, but soon found herself flicking ahead absently. J. K.

K.

Suddenly, it occurred to her what else she'd wanted to look up. *Kingcups!*

Caltha Palustris, the kingcup or marsh marigold, just as she'd thought.

RICHES.

Riches! Riches?

Six of them. Six Riches?

The omnibus rattled across some uneven cobbles at the top of Salisbury Court and Fannie looked up. Workmen were busy unloading a pair of huge new doors from an idling Ruston engine, and struggling to get them into position at the front of the bombed bank.

She wondered where the other five banks were.

Six banks.

Six Riches?

Six kingcups.

Fannie shook her head. A few flowers, a little money changing hands from a gent who was clearly after something else from a beautiful flower girl, that was surely all it was.

This is nonsense, Fannie Douglas. Get a hold of yourself.

But she could not shake her imaginings, nor the queasy doubt they conjured.

What were they with, those kingcups? She racked her brains, but for the life of her could not remember. Three… daffs, she was sure of that. Yes, orange-mouthed jonquils, very distinctive, clashed madly with the kingcups. And… and…a single sprig of greenery. No, she couldn't recall what that was.

Jonquils.

She looked it up. I DESIRE A RETURN OF AFFECTION. That didn't make sense. Plain daffs meant REGARD, but they weren't plain daffs.

She flipped over the page. What else? She scanned the long section on the placement of daffodils on the bosom or collar or wrist, then came to the flower's more mundane meaning: MARCH.

The flower of March. The month just gone.

Three jonquils. And a single sprig of green. If her 'greenery' surmise was correct, one sprig meant 'one'. Three and one. Four, was that four? No, why not have four jonquils then, the Turk had had plenty. Three and one. Thirty-one?

SIX RICHES. MARCH. 31.

The day of the bank robberies.

Six banks attacked on March 31 and this bouquet spelling out exactly that! Had the bouquet been a warning or a confirmation? Green Topper had looked at them, examined them carefully. Had there been a little smile of satisfaction? He'd thanked Lorelei carefully, she'd asked him an innocent question about nasturtiums or something, but he was anything but innocent! He'd been coming back and forth and picking up these strange blooms from the Turk, and little Lorelei was none the wiser! And all the men with their single yellow flowers, that was surely part of the plan...

Her fingers flicked through the pages, automatic as the driver's brass hands on his sticks and levers.

Nasturtium.

PATRIOTISM.

Fannie flinched.

"Excuse me dearie." The woman next to her, who worked on Billingsgate Fish Market by the smell of her, was scowling at her. "Would you mind your elbows?"

"I wouldn't mind, no dear. I wouldn't mind at all!"

The woman looked at her as if she was mad.

Perhaps she was.

As soon as she got to the Market, Fannie would confront Lorelei, tell her of her suspicions, tell her to be on her guard against whatever devilry this was, how these men were corrupting their innocent trade in items of beauty. She'd never heard the like of it! Fannie Douglas, Queen of Covent Garden, would smoke them out for sure.

However, as the bus wound its way past the Law Courts towards Somerset House, she thought better of it.

And then what, Fannie Douglas Queen of Flowers? The girl would think you'd lost your marbles. And who will you tell about this? Will you march into Somerset House and try to get the Coppers or that Brown Derby to listen to you? They'd think you were madder still. You'd end up in Bedlam!

Fannie shivered and tucked away the book in her shawl, getting off at the next stop to clear her head and nostrils.

It must have been later than she thought, because she met the girls coming down from the Market on their trip to the Landing.

"Fannie!"

"Chuckaboo!" Fannie was aware of how her voice was quavering. Her hand trembled as she took Lorelei's arm.

"Are you feeling alright?"

Fannie smiled her widest, fakest smile. "Oh, yes, dearie, don't worry about me. A little gin in my system from last night that's all."

"Was that all you had in your system?" said Clarrie, and the other girls laughed.

On reaching the Landing, Lorelei went straight to the Turk.

This time, Fannie tagged along.

The man eyed her suspiciously. "Who is this?" he asked Lorelei.

"Oh, she's a friend. A very good friend."

The man nodded curtly. Lorelei took her time and picked a selection of somewhat expensive flowers. As she brought out her purse to pay, the vendor's eyes darted left and right, twice to each side. He reached under his cart and brought out a long cardboard box and opened it slightly to show her. "From the Hague, you understand."

Lorelei reached in and took a single bloom from the box. *A black rose!!!!!*

Fannie nearly choked with alarm. "Oh, you shouldn't, my chuckaboo."

"Why ever not?"

"They're...bad luck." She glared at the vendor who scowled in return. "It worries me, trifling with such things."

Lorelei shook her head. Her face looked pinched, a little worn, care lines at the corners of her mouth and eyes. She smiled indulgently. "They're not really black you know, just very, very dark red." She held the bloom up to the light, so the rose's true hue could be discerned.

"Oh, I know that," said Fannie, trying to sound airy but failing miserably, "but they're bad luck all the same. An ill omen, mark my words."

Lorelei seemed to think for a moment, then handed the rose back to the man who took it from her and placed it carefully in the box, which Fannie could see held other flowers, large ones too, though she could not see what they were.

Lorelei counted coins into the man's hand.

Fannie looked at the selection of fine, but run-of-the-mill, flowers Lorelei had on her arm. The coins she'd given the Turk were sufficient for those bunches but only just.

Why hasn't she paid him for that awful rose or whatever else was in that box?!

She glared again at the man as they left.

Fannie felt her stomach begin to tighten. Odd bouquets, that was one thing, but black roses, as ill-omened as they might be, that was an *expensive* gift from the vendor to a fairly new customer. And what else was in that box? Something rarefied, for sure. Her sense of thirty years, forged on the harsh streets of this unforgiving city, come rain come shine, told her something was amiss.

Her nerves did not improve as the day passed.

Lorelei performed her usual artistry with the armful she'd bought, helped the other girls, but the box along with its black rose and other mysterious flowers from the Turk stayed firmly under her rack.

I wonder who that's for, as if I didn't know.

Lunchtime came and went, though Fannie ate nothing, blaming her hangover. In truth, she had no appetite. More than anything, she *had* to know what was in that box.

As if by a miracle, shortly after lunch, Lorelei retrieved the Turk's box, set it on the step behind them, and opened it to examine the contents. Fannie could not help but stare. Beneath the black rose were two enormous stems, with thick stalks, topped with a crown of pointed leaves over a ring of beautiful, orange bell-shaped flowers. Below all this finery lay a single daisy, wrapped in eight small ferns.

Fannie's blood ran cold. This bouquet was no work of artistry, on the contrary, it was unbalanced, almost taunting in its ugliness. This had to mean something.

The flowers were all laid on a grand silken wrap of dark green, tied with a string of faux pearls. Fannie looked away hurriedly as Lorelei closed the box and tucked it under her rack on top of her carpet bag full of accessories. The girl seemed not to have noticed her interest.

Fannie was itching to get out her book and look up these flowers but dared not.

The bell of St Clement Danes tolled two o'clock.

"I need to pop to the conveniences," said Lorelei. "Will you mind my pitch?"

"Of course, dearie. You run along now, I'll keep a beef-eater's watch on your precious blooms, mark my words."

The nearest respectable conveniences were at Garrick Street, which would give Fannie a good quarter of an hour. The moment Lorelei was out of sight, Fannie retrieved the book. There was a whole section on roses. She'd look that up first before searching for the tropical monstrosity.

Rose. Black.

DEATH.

Fannie's heart froze. A strange sensation curled through her gut, as if someone had slipped an eel into her morning porridge.

And what are those huge things?

She flicked through the book so quickly she almost broke its spine, but it fell open at the glossy plates, and there right in front of her was the mystery bloom. Suddenly it came to her. Kew, that's where she'd seen it, and that's where this photograph had been taken.

Fritillaria Imperialis. Native to Turkey and Kashmir. Rare. Grown under glass in the Hague and, of course, at the Royal Botanical Gardens at Kew.

MAJESTY.

The eel turned lazily over and over and over in the pit of her stomach. A black rose. Two of these orange monstrosities. Imperial green silk wrapping them, and pearls. Very regal wrapping, for two regal stems, but nonsense for the forlorn daisy and its attendant ferns.

The voice of the paper boy, across the Market, sounded like a funeral bell. "Read all about it! Read all about it! Queen to ride pneumatic railway!"

Fannie jumped up, found herself light-headed, but ran despite herself, across the uneven flags to the boy, struggling to free a penny from her belt-purse as she did.

The boy saw her, his eyes went wide, he made to flee for

no other reason than any boy might when he saw a large woman barrelling towards him, shouting at him.

"Stop! Stop, you little tyke! I only want to buy a paper!"

The boy halted, a grin appearing on his face. "You scared me, missus. No-one's usually that keen to get the news!"

Fannie pressed a penny into his hand.

"Thank you, missus!"

But she was oblivious to him now, frantically taking in the front-page news.

ROYALS TO LAUNCH NEW PNEUMATIC RAILWAY TRAINS.

HER IMPERIAL MAJESTY QUEEN ALEXANDRINA VICTORIA, THE FOREVER QUEEN, AND HER CONSORT, PRINCE VICTOR, DUKE OF THURINGIA WILL RIDE THE RAILS UPON THE OCCASION OF THE UNVEILING OF MR. BAZALGETTE'S MARVELLOUS MARK II PNEUMATIC TRAINS. APRIL EIGHTH, 1872 WILL BE MARKED AS A MOMENT OF DISTINCTION IN THE EMPIRE OF CENTURIES.

No!

Fannie looked to the western end of the Market but could not see a maroon shawl. She might have five, perhaps even ten minutes, for the queues at the Garrick Street conveniences could be frightful on a busy day.

She ran back to her rack.

"Whatever's the matter?"

"I'm fine, Esther."

"You look as if you've seen a ghost, so you do!"

"Shhhh, I'm fine."

Fannie took a quick look around, but the other girls were busy crowing over a sale Clarrie had just made. She darted under Lorelei's rack and opened the box. More than anything she wanted to destroy this ugly, deadly bouquet, but would never manage to get the huge blooms out of the Market without being seen. She slid the black rose out and stuffed it into her shawl. Then she closed the box again, stowing it exactly as she'd found it.

The eel wriggled through her abdomen.

"Esther, can you watch my pitch for me?"

"Sure, dearie."

"And Lorelei's. She'll be back from Garrick Street soon."

Esther winked. "I have two eyes for the job. Don't you worry."

Fannie took one look towards the Garrick Street end of the Market and made haste towards the Aldwych. There, in an alleyway next to the butcher's was a slops container, a stained metal box six feet long and five high which reeked like the pits of Hell itself. She unwrapped the rose, checked there were no onlookers and threw it over the top of the container into the mess of rotting carcasses and unsaleable bones, skin and offal.

Relief and terror boiled in her.

What have you gone and done, Fannie Douglas?

By the time she returned to the Market, Lorelei was back at her pitch, selling a few stems to a lady with a broad brimmed hat.

Fannie was immediately apologetic. "I got Esther to mind your rack while I went to relieve myself, hope you don't mind, dearie."

Lorelei shook her head, smiled at Esther who grinned toothlessly back at her.

As three o'clock approached, the cold eel started

thrashing in Fannie's belly. She desperately – *desperately* – wanted to visit the conveniences, but was pinned by her dark curiosity, the inevitability of discovery.

The bells of St Clement Danes tolled three.

Green Topper appeared from the Long Lane entrance to the Market. As usual he made straight for Lorelei's pitch.

Lorelei smiled and reached underneath her rack for the cardboard box.

He opened it and looked inside.

Fannie's heart jumped in her chest.

"Is this *it*?" The man's tanned face blanched beneath his spectacles.

Looks more like an albino now… Fannie shook her head from side to side as if this might quiet her treacherous brain.

Lorelei peered into the box, then turned to Fannie. "Where is it?" she hissed.

"I don't know what you mean, dearie."

"The *rose*!!"

Green Topper seemed distracted, looking all around the Market as if he suspected someone might be watching him.

"Oh, that…" Fannie felt herself flush. "I sold it."

"You *sold* it??" echoed Lorelei.

"A gentleman came and wanted something unusual and I thought 'oh, well, my chuckaboo has that lovely rose'." She held out five shillings, all she had, but Lorelei slapped them out of her hand.

Fannie looked down at the coins, into Lorelei's furious face, then turned her head away from her glare. There, right in her eyeline, was Brown Derby, under the arches by the Bow Street entrance, watching intently.

Green Topper looked from one to the other flower girl, his newly pallid brow furrowing above his dark spectacles.

"I had a b-b-black rose for you…" Lorelei looked fearful.

The man's face reddened. "You *had* it? Where is it?"

"My…sister here claims she sold it."

"You *stupid* girl. Do you know what this means?"

"I can run to get you another one," said Lorelei, a note of desperation in her voice.

"Get another one? Of course you can't, *idiot*," he said, in a low hiss. "That's not how this works! Besides, there's no time. This has all been for nothing!"

Green Topper's gaze was fixed on the Bow Street entrance. He hissed, and Fannie looked up, followed his line of sight into the crowd.

A Copper! Time to act, Fannie Douglas, if ever there was. Time to stop this Rad plot!

Green Topper snarled at Lorelei, then turned sharply on his heel and made to leave.

"Oh no you don't!" shouted Fannie and started gesticulating to the blue-uniformed policeman. "Come quick! Come quick! There's mischief afoot!"

Lorelei hissed at her. "What are you doing?"

"Never you mind, my lovely, there's more going on than you know. Dark Lanterns!"

"You fool!" The girl ducked down behind her rack as Fannie continued to holler.

"There he is! There he is! You can't let him get away!" Green Topper had almost made it into the crowd, and Fannie's instinct took over. She grabbed the nearest metal bucket, perhaps a quarter full of water, and flung it towards him.

The bucket narrowly missed Green Topper but thumped into the head of a man right next to him with a sickening thud. The injured man fell like a sack of potatoes, blood spraying from his head wound. The policeman ran towards him and the milling crowd began to tighten as people struggled to get a good look at the fallen man. One woman fainted, another started screaming. One man collided with another in his eagerness and they both fell to the floor, then started fighting. Tension rippled through the crowd.

Fannie tried to catch sight of Green Topper but could not see him through the melee. Her attention was drawn to the slick of bright blood under the feet of those nearest to the man she'd hit. "Oh, sir, I'm terribly sorry!" Fannie's head began to spin.

She looked around for Brown Derby. He was running towards the spot where Green Topper had been, shoving people out of the way as he did so. Behind him, another man, similarly dressed, followed. The policeman was otherwise occupied with the crowd around the injured man. As he reached them, Brown Derby stopped, looked around then directed his colleague to attend to the man directly and had the policeman control the crowd.

"Here, over here! Oh sir, over here!" Fannie looked to Lorelei to help her raise the alarm, but the girl was oblivious, fumbling in her carpet bag. "What are you doing, my lovely? Rescue's on its way!"

"Shut up, you fool! You've ruined everything. *Everything!*"

"What have I ruined? What have I ruined, my chucka-boo, tell me, oh please do I beg you, what has your Fannie gone and done?"

Lorelei ignored her, continuing the search of her bag.

Fannie clasped her hands together in mock-prayer. "You're not thinking of running, are you? These men are here to save you! Your Green Topper, he's a bad 'un!"

On the Market Square, the chaos was spreading. Men were fighting, women screaming or fainting. The police-man blew his whistle for support, adding its warbling, piercing shriek to the hullabaloo.

Fannie shouted at Brown Derby. "It's the flowers! It's the flowers!"

He looked directly at her, puzzlement on his face, cup-ping his hand to his ear. Fannie shouted again. "It's the flowers! The flowers I tell you! They've gulled my poor little Lorelei!"

"Shut up," snapped Lorelei. "You don't know what you're doing."

"I know perfectly well what I'm doing!" She kept gestur-ing towards Brown Derby. "It's all in the Marchioness's book, so it is. *The Language of Flowers*. Well, old Fannie Douglas has it figured. Don't worry, I'll get you out of this pickle, my lovely, we can share a ham at the White Hart tonight, we'll have a laugh about this. We've foiled their plot!"

"*What*?"

Fannie spun round at the hard tone and looked into the girl's bright green eyes. Gone was the sweet and inno-cent beauty. Here was the hard-faced engineer's daughter.

The Radical.

Fannie gasped at the sudden realisation and turned back to Brown Derby.

He was nearly upon them now.

"It's the flowers! The Turk! She doesn't know what she's doing! It's not her! It's not her!" She felt a thump in the small of her back. Her right leg buckled, and she turned to face Lorelei, steadying herself on her rack. The pain in her back was immense, as if a carthorse had kicked her.

Lorelei's eyes were wide, full of sudden tears. The pearl-handled silver derringer trembled in her hand, grey smoke corkscrewing from its right barrel.

Such a little thing. Such a pretty little thing.

Fannie tried to steady herself, but her hand was as cold as the rack itself. Her legs turned to water. The pain in her back had spread to her whole body now. She felt her eyelids tremble as if they were trying to shake her eyes loose. Her scalp itched. Her mouth went dry. She tumbled to the floor, heard her head thud on the flags. Hot liquid began to pool around her.

A shadow loomed over her. She tried to focus on it, but her vision was too blurry.

Then came an almighty crack. She flinched as if she'd been hit by a Hansom going full pelt. Red hot fire burned through her. Had she been kicked by another horse? The sound had come from close by. Her eardrums rang.

She felt big arms around her, wrestler's arms. Her head fell against good wool. Warm, strong arms. Strong brown wool. She could smell cheroot tobacco and the air beyond it. Air filled with laurel, hyacinth and Sweet William from the Sussex Glass and…something else, something strange.

Bitter, deathly.

Is that what gunpowder smells like?

With all her strength, she managed to tip her head over the side of the strong arm cradling it. Then she saw.

Her mouth opened but she could not get the word "chuckaboo" past her dry lips.

Lorelei's green eyes were blank, staring. Brilliant emeralds dulled to scuffed green glass. The side of her face was black, smoky. Black liquid oozed from the pulpy wound.

Not black, not really. Not black. Very, very dark red.

Pale grey smoke rose from the other barrel of Lorelei's gun, which had fallen out of her china doll's hand.

A rare bloom, that one.

Brown Derby's embrace was surprisingly soft for a wrestling man.

She could sleep, in his strong arms.

Always ill-omened, Fannie Douglas, always ill-omened, a black rose...

ΨΨΨΨΨΨ

THE UNRULY CUCKOO CLOCK

"So, YOU ARE attached to the Special Branch of Scotland Yard, are you, er, Inspector?"

The homeowner in question, one Mr Harrison, was attempting a technique known as 'rapport-building', Max's training suggested. In this case the man was using coarse general knowledge of the workings of the police to pretend a level of sophistication it was clear he did not possess, judging by the array of pretentious Middle Class gewgaws neatly arranged on the long table in the tiled hallway.

"*Invigilator.*" Max sighed. This was a common occurrence in his profession.

"Oh, yes, of course, I'm terribly sorry." Harrison was a beetle-like man of perhaps forty-five, bereft of whiskers and moustache. Clearly an accountant, banker, actuary or, worse, insurance man. "Look, here's Cecily with tea."

The maidservant wheeled in a brass-plated Vienna cart – another terrible Middle Class affectation – bearing a frightful Spode teapot, matching service and a silver cake-stand bearing a selection of decidedly Middle Class fancies and crustless sandwiches.

"Very kind," said Max, without emotion. Emotions were the very devil, in his view. An experienced detective invigilator in the Constabulary of Chronological Affairs – commonly known as the Time Police, though never within the Constabulary itself – had no room for emotion. Emotion led to irrationality. Emotion led to mistaken judgements. Emotion was *imprecise*. Imprecision was the greatest crime of all.

"Punch fancy?" Harrison poured tea and indicated the cake-stand. "Cook is a marvel with quince. We've several bushes in the garden." His voice quavered slightly.

This man is nervous, thought Max.

Despite himself, Max was tempted by the fancy but declined, sipped instead at his tea. Citizenry Relations was a minor part of his role, but Max's firm view was that full adherence to the principles of English Proper Time was more likely where its true custodians – the Constabulary – treated the citizenry with politeness. Tea was politeness. Cake was indulgence, leading to emotion and so forth down the track to complete *chaos*.

"Before we inspect the errant chronometer," said Max, adopting his formal Constabulary terminology, "you might tell me something of its history."

"Ah yes." Harrison was halfway through a quince fancy. A few crumbs fell from his mouth down the front of his machine-print waistcoat.

Max, through force of will, prevented his lip from curling disdainfully. Crumbs, the very *acme* of imprecision…

Harrison replaced the remaining half of the confection on his plate. "I believe my grandfather acquired the clock in Prague."

"City of clocks." Max nodded. It might be venerable then, custom-made certainly.

"I-I-indeed," stammered Harrison. "Anyway, Grand-papa brought it back to England via Paris, where I believe he had its oscillator replaced."

"*Replaced*?" Max felt disdain rising once more.

"Yes. He was French on his mother's side, my great-*grandmère*, and had always had an affection for French engineering."

Max harrumphed. "This may be the reason for its mal-function."

"Oh, do you think so?"

Max engaged *Citizenry Relations* once again. He should not offend the French blood flowing through the man's veins. "French machinery is customarily of superb design," he said, carefully, "though our experience is that what it may achieve in style, it loses in reliability." He pronounced the last word, one of the watchwords of the Constabulary, with emphasis and not a little reverence.

"Oh," said the beetle.

Max smiled tightly. "Do go on. What is its mainte-nance history?"

"Well, I am of course cognisant of my role as a Custo-dian of Time…"

Max fought hard to stop his eyes rolling. *Why did we choose to indulge the Middle Class with that nonsense?*

"…and so, it has been our practice, Mrs Harrison and I, to make sure that at the first sign of trouble, or variance, we attend the Clockwork Clockmaker in Ossuary Row in the City of London."

"Very prudent. And how do you detect any…variances?" This was a standard Constabulary question. Any owner of a fine timepiece or striking clock should be aware of their responsibilities, but modernity had encouraged a certain laxity, anathema to the maintenance of English Proper Time.

"Oh. My wife's brother is a parson in Woolwich. It is his practice to adjust his own fob-watch by the Imperial Clock outside the Greenwich Observatory once every week. When he comes for tea on a Sunday, we verify all our timepieces via his pocket watch."

Max nodded. "That is a practical system," he conceded, though the kind of timepieces which would be taken for such a ritual might have lost or gained a second by the time their owners returned to the Pneumatic Underground Railway station at Blackheath, never mind made it all the way here to Chiswick. Still, weekly adjustments were the backbone of English Proper Time, and he suspected few adhered to the advised regimen. Max was mildly impressed. "So, Mr Harrison, when did this malfunction first occur?"

"As I explained in my letter…" Harrison held a copy out to Max, who gave a curt nod but did not take the sheet, "…it does not appear to be a malfunction as such."

"Let me be the judge of that," said Max, stiffly.

"That is to say," Harrison jumped back in, "that it keeps perfectly proper time, by my brother-in-law's pocket watch. It is, however, *changing*."

Max had read Harrison's letter, the original of which was neatly folded inside his jacket, but scarcely believed a word of it. He presumed Mrs Harrison had written it, so hysterical was it, so florid the language. "*Changing* you say? Perhaps we should inspect it."

Harrison breathed a huge sigh of relief and jumped up from his seat. "Oh, yes, this way. It's in the drawing room. I did not want to risk trying to move it, though my good lady wife pleaded with me to do so. She will not enter that room now, which vexes her mightily as she is something of a Bridge aficionado. She holds a ladies' party every Wednesday, you see, but will not move her party to the smoking room on account of her dislike of the wallpaper in that room. She feels it too 'masculine' for a feminine company…"

Max sighed as Harrison wittered on. *Citizenry Relations…* what a very imprecise notion that was, in itself, given the propensity of said citizenry to jibber-jabber about all manner of twaddle.

The clock hung in the generous alcove to the right of what even Max had to concede was an impressive fireplace of black marble with a grand pair of Prussian eagles on the overmantel.

"Grandpapa brought this fireplace back from Königsberg," explained Harrison. "He was an energetic collector."

"So I see," said Max. "It's a fine piece."

"And this is the clock."

Max drew in a breath, despite himself. In his twenty-five years in the Constabulary, he had never seen the like.

The clock was a common enough pendulum-regulated chalet style Hunt Clock, or *Jagdstück*, a well-made example, constructed in wood and topped with a stag's head surrounded by crossed oak leaves. Max hated Hunt Clocks, not least because of the infernal bird which lived behind a trap door above the face and sounded every hour with an increasingly irksome fanfare of "*cuckoo!*" thanks to the miniature bellows concealed in its 'nest'.

Something had been done to this one, however. The right face of the machine, almost half the clock, was encrusted with glittering parts. Upon closer inspection, these revealed themselves to be watch-parts: springs, levers, wheels, fingers, pinions, correctors, winding stems, as well as a few tiny dials which looked incongruous, a scattering of porcelain eyes across a brass field.

"What on earth have you done to this, man?"

"Mercy me!" said Harrison, more beetle-like than ever now in his frantic denial. "I haven't done anything to it! I came down one morning and noticed one tiny cog upon it. I tried to remove it, but it would not budge. By lunchtime that day, there were half a dozen parts apparent. I obtained a watchmaker's catalogue to try to identify them, to see if there might be some kind of clue there but could not make heads nor tails of it. Finally, I thought it might be some kind of *disease*. I fancied I could see this new portion moving, fraction-ally. My wife suggested I may be experiencing some kind of seizure and had me take a powder, but it made no odds. I began to avoid the room entirely, so per-turbed was I. At that point I determined I should write to the Constabulary."

Max, who had regained his previous calm, took out his magnifying glass, removed it from its black velvet pouch and began to inspect the clock. He began at the bottom, where one of the weights still retained its pinecone shape, but the other had been replaced by something else entirely, an angular construction almost like a lady's necklace of a peculiarly Gothic design, with what looked like a death's-head at its centre.

"Look at the top, at the deer," bubbled Harrison from behind him. The man was cowering, clearly petrified.

Max obliged and examined the miniature stag's head which crowned the clock. Half of the stag's imagined skin was missing, along with its left eye, left-side lips and one nostril. Instead, the eye socket, teeth and skull were exposed in livid ivory. Max recoiled slightly. Whoever had done this was an artist of the first measure, albeit one with a ghoulish sensibility. It was exquisitely detailed, entirely as if a tiny stag had been killed for the purposes of building this strange device.

"And then the face," murmured Harrison. "What is *that*?"

The porcelain dial of the clock had been partly altered also, in addition to both clock hands. The numbers on the changed half of the dial were now hard black, machine-struck Gothic, in contrast to the lighter, hand-painted characters on the other side. The hour hand resembled an especially vicious pike, while what looked like a tiny brass gargoyle, such as might be found along the edge of the roof of a medieval cathedral, clung to the tip of the ornate black blade of the minute hand.

"And the cuckoo?" Max pushed his glass slowly in the direction of the cuckoo's nest.

Harrison quailed and took to the Queen Anne chair beside him. "I dare not…" He gripped the arms of the chair so hard his knuckles turned white.

Max looked at his own watch, a chronometer of the first order, set to Imperial Time of course. The cuckoo clock was in exact step with it.

Exact.

How is that possible?

Imperial Time was the preserve of the Greenwich Observatory, the Military, the Constabulary and the First Family alone. There was no way a man of Harrison's position, for all the interesting antiquities he seemed to own, could afford it. Of course, it might be mere coincidence. Nothing could be ruled out, at this stage, but Max did not believe in coincidence, especially not of the 'mere' variety.

"I believe this to be a defective piece," he said calmly, "and I will have to remove it when I am done inspecting it."

"Very good." Harrison seemed relieved.

"Consequently, the time it marks is also defective. I am compelled to force it to chime."

Harrison nodded, though his permission was neither sought nor necessary. He then shuddered and looked away, cringing.

Max took a slim brass rod from his breast pocket and gently moved the minute hand to twelve. The trap door above the face – now, Max noted, a replica of the circular steel door of a bank vault – opened with a click and its occupant burst forth. Max staggered back a couple of steps despite himself. The tiny brass demon, no other word for it, which had taken the place of the cuckoo gave an ugly hiss and flapped its gruesome brass bat wings twice before disappearing.

But the worst, the very worst thing, was that after the demon had disappeared, the hands whirred around as if possessed, resetting the clock to its previous time.

Imperial Time.

"This must be monkeyshines," said Max under his breath. But this could be no prank. It was impossible.

Impossible. A chill made its way from the base of Max's skull to his extremities. He began to perspire, cool moisture springing from every pore on his body. His heart hammered in his chest, his breaths became shorter.

No. He must contain himself. He took two, three deep breaths, closed his eyes until a measure of uneasy calm took hold.

"Look closer, around the face," whispered Harrison. The man was curled up in a ball in his chair now.

Max took up his magnifying glass again. He was aware he was shaking, almost imperceptibly, but definitely. He peered carefully at the clock to the right side of its corrupted face. As he looked, a tiny gearwheel appeared as if out of nowhere, extending the boundary of brass over the wood below. But then, something else caught his eye. "Are those...?" he said, mostly to himself.

"Tentacles," said Harrison, with a shudder. "They're tentacles!"

Sure enough, Max noted three clumps of golden tentacles extruding from the body of the clock, slim, evil-looking appendages equipped with tiny suckers as one might find on an octopus or squid. His mouth went dry. "What is this devilry?"

"I don't know!" wailed Harrison.

Then, as Max looked through the glass still, he noticed that each occurrence of the golden tentacles was in gentle motion, undulating, curling at the tips, suckers expanding and contracting microscopically.

Max recoiled once again. "What is this *devilry*!?" he repeated. Twenty-five years in the Constabulary of Chronological Affairs had not prepared him for this. "I..." he started but found himself lost for words.

"What do we *do*?" Harrison pleaded.

"I…we…must confiscate this…thing," said Max, correcting himself on the basis that there was no way on God's Green Earth that he was undertaking this task on his own, unprepared. He would return to headquarters immediately and share his findings with the Chief. This clock would be destroyed after a full examination, he was sure of that. Invigilators would be despatched to Prague and to Paris, and he would make sure he was one of them.

They returned to the dining room where Max sat down. He levered two, three, four small cubes of sugar into his tea and stirred it swiftly while Harrison watched transfixed. Max took it down in one swig. It would steady his nerves until he could get back to the Constabulary.

"You must seal and lock this room until my return," Max instructed as they exited to the hallway. The maidservant was standing there, ready to open the door. Had she been earwigging? He could not take the chance. "You – and your household – must not breathe a word of this," he said, gravely. "If you have already imparted any information on this phenomenon you *must* tell me, under the Chronological Security Act of 1854, to whom you spoke. We will then undertake what we call Contact Tracing whereupon anyone you have spoken to will be contacted and warned of the damaging nature of such infectious rumour. The penalty for non-compliance or wilful inaccuracy is up to four years' hard labour."

Harrison and the maid both gulped. "No…nobody, except my wife," said Harrison, finally. He and the maid looked at one another, wide-eyed.

Max sighed. "You will need to speak to your wife, and you will provide me, by secure telegram, the names and addresses of anyone she has spoken to about this. Do you understand?" He handed the man a pad of secure telegram paper with the insignia of the Constabulary of Chronological Affairs at the top of each page.

Harrison looked at the pad as if it might explode in his hands. He nodded.

"This is a most serious case," said Max. "If you provide me with the requisite names and addresses, I will recommend that you are *not* prosecuted for possession of an illegal chronometer," he added, to Harrison's evident relief. "But this must go no further, do you understand me?"

Harrison and maid both nodded.

Max left and made to hail a Hansom in the street. An automatic cabriolet arrived, and he climbed aboard. He preferred automatics. Their brass drivers asked no questions and communicated no information to others. If he had his way, every human cabbie in London would be out of a job, simply on security grounds.

The cab pulled away from the Harrison residence, joined the traffic on Ellesmere Road, and began the half hour journey back to headquarters.

Max was consumed by an unearthly unease, the like of which he had never felt. The dead stag, the self-conjuring gearwheels, the waving tentacles, that was all very unsettling. But the thing which had perturbed him most, chilled him to the very core, was that the thing marked Imperial Time.

Imperial Time! *Self-generated* Imperial Time!!

No Middle Class timepiece was capable of generating time of any kind, never mind Imperial Time. Imperial

Time was uniquely accurate, the product of the Greenwich Atom, provided via glass conduits cast in copper sheaths to the Engines themselves and no others. Imperial Time was the province of the military and the railways alone. Even the chronometers in the Imperial Palace required daily adjustment to keep pace.

That idea that this modest, ugly *jagdstück* could self-correct to Imperial Time was impossible, *uncountenanceable*. God forbid there were *other* mutant clocks on the mantelpieces of England or lurking in hallway cabinetry.

Max shuddered at the thought. He felt in his pocket for a capsule of Dr Havelock's Democratic Nerve Restorative and swallowed it dry.

The Hansom conveyed him rapidly to the Aldwych. Not quickly enough, he felt.

After all, as the motto of the Constabulary of Chronological Affairs clearly stated, Time was of the essence…

ΨΨΨΨΨΨ

BATTLESHIP JUNK

THE TWO MEN walked down the metalled sand-strewn path towards the tallest construction in all London. Barnaby looked up at the four slim, brick towers, impossible amounts of olive drab canvas strung between them, then at the huge barricades. A cordon of matelots, cutlasses in their belts, rifles slung across their backs, stood chatting, smoking.

Guard duty. Painfully boring until it wasn't, according to his father, a proper military man if ever there was one, sinews turned to iron by those frigid nights in the hills of the Northwest Frontier, heart turned to iron by the family he had never wanted, and especially the son who showed no interest in a career in the Services.

"Are you sure this is *strictly* necessary, William?" Barnaby heard his voice quaver, as it was prone to do when confronted with large quantities of military *matériel*. Not for the first time, he questioned whether he was cut out to be Grand Secretary of Homeland Surety. But as with so many of the other ministers in this Tory administration, he'd had little choice over the posting. Nothing to do but buckle up and get on with the job. Another of his father's little gems.

"Oh yes, very much so." The Admiral – William – had been in Barnaby's house at Clifton Academy and was one of the few fellows Barnaby had managed to keep in close touch with over the years. He tapped his unlit cigar absently against his leg to settle the leaves then apparently thought better of smoking it and slid it into his left breast pocket behind the glittering row of medals. "We can't have wandering members of the general public catching sight of it before we're ready. And we need to protect against sabotage."

"Are those *Maxim guns*?" Barnaby pointed at the crabbed black guns squatting on wheeled mounts which punctuated the barricades at precisely regular intervals.

"Yes, yes they are, Barnaby." Unlike Sir Barnaby Ridge, Admiral Sir William Fortescue-Roberts positively revelled in armaments of all kinds. "Maxim Twos, in point of fact. Twice the fire-rate of the original."

Barnaby looked to the sky above Battersea Park. "Dear Lord, save us. Who are you expecting to assault this position, the whole Prussian army?"

The Admiral ignored the jibe. "Perhaps you would like a closer look at the item in question?"

"I suppose I better had, given the dent this thing has put in my budget." Barnaby suppressed a sigh. "Lead on, William."

The Admiral gave a courteous nod of his tricorne and they began the hundred-yard walk to the base of the North Tower. It took them some time to traverse the ranks of barricades due to the amount of saluting that had to go on. They moved past the guns, past the black coils of razored wire, past ranks of drab-clad militia with bully clubs sprinkled with brightly dressed marines carrying the latest machine pistols, until they came finally to a line of Highland shock troops in full regalia, kilts, black and red diced hose and feather bonnets. If they felt any excitement or curiosity at the visit of two such august personages, it did not show on the men's faces.

"Is this all *really* necessary?"

The Admiral stopped. "I must confess myself surprised, Barnaby. This is the greatest project of our age, a project for which you have budgetary responsibility. I would have thought you might have recognised how sensitive this is, how important to the Empire."

Barnaby wished he had consulted the designs when this project had first been agreed upon, but had decided not to, officially on security grounds but in reality, on the grounds of personal animus and frank disinterest. He had had no input whatever to the decision and as such had no personal stake in it, unlike William. Barnaby was there to ensure it was delivered on time and on budget, nothing more, he had told himself. Now, he regretted not taking a closer look at its blueprints. "I know how important this is to the Prime Minister."

The Admiral looked at him askance but seemed unable to quibble with his answer. "Hmm, well, yes," was all he could manage.

They resumed their walk.

Barnaby was not the greatest adherent of Steam Doctrine as a universal philosophy, but, given his advancing years, was very grateful the Navy had demanded steam elevators to convey men and supplies from the base of two of the towers to the cantilevered galleries from where inspections could be carried out. The Navy had wanted four elevators – in the name of Jupiter! – but he had pared this down to two on budgetary grounds, and so two had been installed at opposite corners. There were many grumbles in high places, because the Navy was not accustomed to being denied, ever. But good accounting principles were just that, and budgets were not unlimited.

The Admiral waved his guest into the North Elevator. A matelot stood in the steel cage, ready to close the concertina mesh door and operate the large brass lever. Both passengers held onto the thick brass handrails as they ascended, steam hissing from the engine below them, but the matelot stood unsupported, his sturdy legs parted slightly.

The elevator rattled and rocked as they went up, which Barnaby found to be less uncomfortable than he feared, rather like the rocking of a railway carriage, and soon, they were at gallery level. The matelot opened the thick steel mesh which had contained them and pushed open the metal door facing them.

"Is that – " started Barnaby, peering at the door.

"From a ship?" finished the Admiral. "Yes, yes it is." He smiled like the cat who got the cream.

"Ah, how…ingenious."

"Waste not, want not." The Admiral inclined his head slightly and swept his hand in front of the door, encouraging his guest to go first. "I think you will be impressed with what we've accomplished using what we call *battleship junk*." He pronounced the words with a mix of derision and resignation, such as might a cook forced to perform culinary miracles with inadequate pans.

"Battleship junk?"

"It's exactly what it sounds like." The Admiral helped himself to a pinch of snuff and sneezed almost instantly. "We've had to have some pieces cast fresh, but even they were formed from melted armour plating for the most part. Finer steel cannot be had, though recasting is not ideal for tensile strength according to our engineers. As for the rest, follow me, Barnaby, and we can take a look."

They moved along a broad passageway whose sturdy planking displayed many scratches and scores on its heavy varnish.

Barnaby pointed at the floor. "More...battleship junk?"

"Yes indeed." The Admiral smiled. "Budgets and all that."

Barnaby did not rise to the bait.

They approached another metal door. It swung open, revealing a matelot on the other side who saluted smartly.

"Here we are." The Admiral's introduction was entirely superfluous.

Barnaby gaped. "My..." was all he could manage.

"Quite impressive, I think you'll agree."

"I..."

The device was close to two hundred feet tall. Barnaby had overheard two of his under-secretaries gabbling excitedly about it, but he had dismissed it as a veritable tall tale. And yet here it was: two hundred feet of steel and brass, rubber and battleship deck planking.

It had the build of a heavyweight prizefighter, thick across the shoulders and with arms too long for its body, like those of an ape. It was difficult to see the hands from here, but they looked overlarge. Rather than two legs, it had three, two in front and one behind, each as thick as a battleship funnel – looked as if they *were* battleship funnels – for their whole length. Its head appeared to have been constructed from two turrets one on top of the other, which gave it a fearsome countenance, presumably the architect's express intent. Each turret's guns were absent. In their place on the top turret were two massive searchlights, as one might find on a lighthouse, while the bottom turret's gun mounts had been cut out entirely and a command bridge installed with glass panes set in frames of the brightest brass, giving the impression of a grinning mouth. Atop the head was a ring of smaller turrets bearing an assortment of Maxims, carronades and Armstrong guns, and above them, a complex array of brass signalling equipment and several flagpoles.

The most peculiar – and, to the mind of the Grand Secretary, troubling – aspect of the device were the two turrets in the centre of its midsection. These were very much still armed, with short barrelled naval guns. He gulped. Scotland Yard had signed off on *this,* for use in the streets of London? Below the turrets, another ring of cupolas with Maxims and sniper stations ringed the lower mid-section of the contraption.

"Naval guns…" he started, but both he and William knew it was far too late to offer any objections.

"Some call it a Vaucanson Engine," said the Admiral, entirely ignoring his colleague's pallid protestation. "I find that description unsatisfying, and decidedly Frenchified."

"They are our *allies.*"

The Admiral harrumphed. He had not been a fan of the Le Havre Treaty, along with most of the Navy, but these days the international affairs of the Empire were settled more by diplomacy and less at the end of a steel barrel and so he had been forced to be polite to the French, at least publicly. "One Cambridge professor said it was more like a Hephaestus Table," he said. "Though I concede that my classical education is scant at best, I fear if it sounds absurd to me, then it would surely sound absurd to the citizenry."

"I agree," said the Grand Secretary. His mind reeled. How on God's Green Earth had he let this thing proceed? He fumbled for some mundanity to fill the yawning void which threatened to open up at the centre of the conversation. "So, what have you settled on by way of...er...a description for this...um...engine?"

The Admiral leaped on the opportunity to expound. "Some of my colleagues are enamoured of the term 'mecha'. I favour 'giant automaton'." He paused, as if marshalling a greater point. "Although its designation serves as a description of the device, of which we may decide to construct more should the necessity arise, my device's *name* will be what begins its story. I daresay that it may also become something of a generic term, if indeed more are planned." He looked intently at Barnaby as military men often did when forced to converse with mere civilians. "A single war machine of any kind always has the note of vulnerability, all eggs in one basket, so to speak."

"War machine?"

Too late, Barnaby, too, too late.

The Admiral turned on him, as if some grand scheme had finally crystallised. His eyes were bright, his face flushed with excitement. "If we are to put down the

Radicals once and for all, I recommend we construct more automata such as this. Now that we have the way of it, we should be able to build them close to shipyards with relative ease and, coincidentally, close to the hotbeds of the Radical movement. We can begin with the Clyde, Mersey and Tyne though I myself would like to see one on the Severn, protecting the bridge perhaps or on patrol in Bristol itself."

"Bristol?" Barnaby thought of the exclusive private boarding school where he had first met the Admiral, some forty years prior. The school, which had produced some of England's finest, the school which had fallen into scandal and ruin, the school which had been demolished to make way for Lord Brunel's beautiful suspension bridge, from which one had an uninterrupted view of one of the Empire's finest port cities. The idea of this thing planting itself in the harbour to terrorise his beloved Bristol chilled the Grand Secretary to his very marrow.

"Do you not see the potential, Barnaby? We have the opportunity to use these to install, finally, Law and Order at the heart of the Empire, and then in turn across all the Colonies. My architects have concluded that automata may be too vulnerable for a modern battlefield, but against union men, rascals, and even Swing mobs, they will dominate the streets."

"Shock and Awe," said the Grand Secretary, softly. The name of the policy outlined by the Prime Minister to deal with the Rads. "I see that now."

"And thanks to all those damnable naval treaties, we have a great deal of battleship junk." The Admiral grimaced sourly. "I am confident that having constructed this automaton successfully, others will be markedly more economical. We shall begin field tests next week, right here in the park. All will be welcome. Shock and Awe begins with the power of the word, and rest assured the word will travel the length and breadth of the land very quickly. The Radicals will be quaking when they hear her name."

"Which is?" The Grand Secretary realised he had forgotten to enquire of the Admiral until now, lost as he seemed in his revelries of power.

"*Dreadnought*," said the Admiral.

The Grand Secretary sighed and let his head drop as his stomach turned over, knowing that the principle which had held this Empire of Centuries together – government by consent – would vanish with *Dreadnought's* first step into the world.

ΨΨΨΨΨΨ

ᴛʜᴇ ᴄLOCKWORK ᴄLOCKMAKER

Iꜰ ʏᴏᴜ ᴀʀᴇ one of those fortunate enough to possess a timepiece so finely constructed as to require the attentions of only the finest craftsman, and if that timepiece were to malfunction – perhaps begins to lose time or fails to chime as expected – you will know where it needs to be taken: south on Kingdom Street, past the automatic cab rank, make a left by the fountain where urchins compete for your loose change, along Ropemaker Street, under the iron bridge which carries the pneumatic overground and across the intersection into Colony Row, making a sharp left after the shop selling fine lace, and finally, taking yourself into the irregular jitty known as Ossuary Lane.

Halfway down, tucked between what was once a moneylender's house on the one side and what is still a hostelry of somewhat ill repute on the other, is the dusty establishment belonging to the Clockwork Clockmaker.

Upon a visit such as this, occasioned by chronological malfunction serious enough to warrant the attentions of the Clockmaker, you will, most likely, not concern yourself with peering in through the appallingly grimed panes at the stacked shelves of grandiose and commonplace timepieces the Clockmaker has – apparently – fashioned during his long career in the palaces of Europe. These items are not for sale in any event. The Clockmaker has no need of money, although the sound of falling gold pleases him, as you will know.

You will have brought with you a walking stick, or some equivalent item of ebony, rosewood or oak, most likely, with a polished brass cap or animal head carved in bone. You will know to rap three times on the right side of the doorframe exactly six inches below the lintel, as this will cause the door to open for you.

You will know to convey your errant timepiece to the small, round mahogany table and place it upon the bright green baize before the Clockmaker himself. You will be aware it is not customary to look at the Clockmaker as you deposit your gold guinea onto the brass plate atop the small cherrywood box, which is positioned towards the rear of the tabletop, although it is not forbidden either – who would stop you from so doing?

Indeed, if you have sent a trusted manservant on this errand in your stead you might even *encourage* the fellow to take a look so that he may be struck in appreciation of what it truly means to own a fine timepiece, one that demands the attentions of this unique engineer. If you are of what one may term an *imaginative* cast of mind, you may fancy that this may provoke in your good servant the ambition to elevate his position so as to perhaps one day be in possession of a qualifying chronograph himself, appropriate desire being the cornerstone of societal progress, after all.

You will advise your manservant that he should expect to hear nothing from the Clockmaker in the way of speech during the assessment process. Indeed, you will be careful to warn him not to misconstrue any clicking, whirring or any other mechanical sound as an attempt to communicate. You might also perhaps advise him not to stare too deeply into what he may imagine are the Clockmaker's eyes, for he may find prolonged exposure to this 'gaze' disconcerting.

You will most *definitely* advise your man that he need not instruct the Clockmaker about his business. The Clockmaker will most certainly know what is amiss with the item.

Your man will hear a single chime, indicating that the assessment is completed and, if the commission is accepted, the gold guinea will drop into the cherrywood box. The door will open automatically, and your man will leave without delay.

In the *very* unlikely event of the commission not being accepted, the door will not open. In that case, your man will need to turn and retrieve the defective item and the guinea. At this point, the door will open, and he must leave. In this case, your item has been deemed irreparable and must be taken without delay to the Office of Defective Chronology, where a certificate will be issued.

Ah, but perhaps your good lady wife fancies to retain such a pretty item, to convert to a jewel case, perhaps, or some kind of display cabinet? Dissuade her of this sentimental nonsense! Failure to present your defective device at the Office of Defective Chronology will result in the prompt attendance at your address of a representative of the Constabulary of Chronological Affairs. Your redundant item will be destroyed, you will be fined, and you will suffer such grave dishonour in society that your ownership of a fine chronograph of any kind will henceforth be carefully proscribed.

Time, you will know, is *not* to be trifled with.

As an upstanding citizen, you will be fully cognisant with the different qualities of Time as managed within this Empire of Centuries.

Imperial Time – the highest grade of time, naturally – is, as you will no doubt know, calculated by the Greenwich Observatory, an output of the Greenwich Atom, the most powerful and unique Engine on Earth.

Imperial Time ensures land trains depart and arrive when they must and directs its divine force towards the perfectly regularised operation of the pneumatic railways. Imperial Time dictates the movement of air- and seaships. It describes the movement of every battleship's shell as it launches itself towards our enemies and it confines the Land Artillery to pinpoint accuracy during times of war, minimising collateral civilian casualties. Imperial Time lends its precision to the workings of the Mother of Parliaments, and, perhaps most importantly of all, ensures that Afternoon Tea at the Palace always – *always* – takes place at 4pm precisely.

In this greatest of world empires, precision is all. Without it, accurate time could not be shipped to the colonies, could not be sold to the supplicant kingdoms and caliphates who are so desirous of this most unique and luxurious commodity.

Imperial Time is the exclusive preserve of our glorious First Family, the Diplomatic Service, the Aristocracy, the Military and men of science, as well as those wealthy enough to afford not simply its installation, but its continuous upkeep.

You, the owner of a clock of quality, are a bulwark of English Proper Time, the backbone of the common Empire. You will have purchased your timepiece from a reputable maker with the requisite Royal Warrant or have perhaps inherited an item with the proper accreditations. English Proper Time lacks the exactitude of Imperial Time but provides you with a reliable and appropriate time which requires little upkeep and only very occasional repair such as the Clockmaker provides.

You share this commodity with the Mercantilium and with our great universities and museums, with our medical practitioners, lawyers and men of the cloth. Your own timepiece itself forms part of a great network of accredited machines whose influence will be felt by your understairs servants, your children and by every tradesman who visits your home.

English Proper Time allows you to convene and arrive at meetings promptly, allows you to make prudent estimations so that you never miss a train and marks you out as a Person of Distinction.

You, dear Citizen, are a *Custodian* of Time.

Imagine where we would we be if Street Time held sway! Imagine what calamaties would occur if the Empire relied upon the slapdash figuring of time by the tinker or flowergirl via the position of sun or the height of the river or of a sundial on a wall. Imagine if affairs were conducted according to the kind of inferior timepieces purchased on the Portobello Road market or in the gin-palaces of Covent Garden.

What a *petrifying* thought!

Poor time *corrodes*. It is anathema to the health and proper functioning of civilised society. It is the enemy of Order and of Empire.

Your manservant may not understand this. Lodging doubtless in a louse-ridden corner of our great Capital City where time is not properly valued or understood, say Bethnal Green, perhaps, or Waterloo, he may content himself with a moderately priced machine-pressed chronograph, perhaps adorned with gilded paste figures or gaudily Japanned panels. In all likelihood he will not *care* if it loses or gains seconds here and there, a minute every week or a fiver a month. When he espies any default, he will count on his own crude judgement to correct it – incorrectly – by *hand*, the grime of his fingers causing its machinery to become soiled and err still further. He will not oil it, will not clean its moving parts, and it will become ever more inaccurate.

If time were in the possession of his class, we would be in *chaos*.

You, fortunate Custodian, you can be assured that regular and careful attentions directed towards your own machine, and your adherence to the traditions of Excellence in Time, regulated by the Constabulary, will be enough to prevent us slipping into oblivion.

For all his modest surroundings, for the gloom, the apparent desuetude of his environment, the Clockwork Clockmaker is a precious relic, a reminder to us that we are all dependent, at some points of our existence, on a single lynchpin.

If you are of good fortune to possess, or to have come

into possession via some generous legacy, a chronometer worthy of his attention, dear Citizen, know that you are one of the Chosen.

God Save The Queen.

ΨΨΨΨΨΨ

The SECRETS of ART

"**T**URNER!!"

The boy, startled, wobbled at the very top of the old wooden ladder. "Monsieur Corneille?"

Corneille held his breath. The boy swayed first to the left, then to the right, grabbed for the shelf to steady himself but in the process sent a box frame skittering off. They both watched as the picture fell without turning and landed on its back on the worn boards below. There was a frightful dull sound as the glass broke into a thousand pieces, most of which stayed in the frame, crashing onto the work it contained.

"Oh! Oh!" Turner's face turned an impossible Carmine.

Corneille rolled his eyes. "I should dock your pay for such incompetence!" He looked down at the frame, miraculously intact despite its precipitous descent. Gertrude Pinnock's 'Lancelot in the Lake' was now swamped with tiny chunks of glass as if the water he lay in had frozen over him. "But then I have always hated this painting, this tragedy of *derivation*, the very *nadir* of disappointment."

The boy hovered on the edge of relief.

Corneille waved his hand airily. "I shall tell Lady

Gertrude that her masterwork burned to ash in an unfortunate easel fire."

The boy, clearly relieved, began to descend.

"Turner!" said Corneille, jabbing his cane at the boy. "When I send you to mount this ladder, it is not for the *sport* of it. When I require of you the use of a ladder it is because I wish you to retrieve an item for which I have the *need*. Kindly regain the summit of this ladder, precarious as it might be, and do not return to me until you have the container of Coromandel kauri gum!"

"Yessir!"

Corneille shook his head. Good assistants were hard to find, yet common boys were ten a penny. Turner would do until he found a replacement for…replacement for…no, the memory was still too painful. Corneille shuffled back behind the counter and watched the boy searching through the dusty array of jars on the very top shelf of the stack.

He looked at his watch. A little past eleven.

A helmeted policeman walked by on the pavement outside Louis Corneille et Fils, London's premier establishment for all the needs of the professional artist.

Corneille's heart tightened in his chest. He felt in his waistcoat pocket to retrieve the enamelled case, thumbed out one of the silvered pills, reached for the glass mug of elderflower and quince *tisane* beside him and swallowed Dr Havelock's Democratic Nerve Restorative with a slight wince.

The policeman stopped, peering through the window at the wooden cases with their serried ranks of oil paints.

It was nothing. This was nothing. It was a colourful display. Anyone might look at it. Anyone. Anyone at all.

Including a policeman. This meant nothing. No policeman could possibly…

Turner banged the ceramic jar down on the counter, snapping Corneille out of his anxiety.

"You *idiot*!"

"This not what you wanted, Monsieur Corneille?"

"Yes of course it is what I wanted! Does not the label proclaim it to be 'Kauri Gum'?"

Turner looked at the dog-eared label, his mouth moving as he read the words. "Yeah, yeah it does. I think."

"It does," Corneille conceded. "But have I not told you one *thousand* times that you are required to treat all glass and ceramic with care? Now go and clean up the mess you have made of Lady Gertrude's witless perversion of the travails of the sainted Lady Nimuë." He reached behind the counter for a chocolate to take away the bitter aftertaste of Dr Havelock's renowned remedy. "In a spirit of equally saintly *largesse*, I have decided not to take anything from your pay by way of recompense for the broken glass."

Turner sighed with relief. His normal complexion – Flake White with a hint of Roman Ochre – was beginning to reassert itself on the acne-scarred canvas of his thin face.

"However!" Corneille picked up and pointedly replaced the jar of kauri gum gently on the mahogany countertop, flashing a terse smile as he did so. "I will require you to assist me this evening. That will discharge your debt to me while preserving your salary."

The boy looked crestfallen. Presumably he had arranged to meet his urchin friends at the Walthamstow electric dog track or somesuch. "I… I mean I don't mind helping you out of course, Monsieur Corneille, sir, it's just that…"

"Yes?"

Turner nodded his head out of the window towards the British Museum opposite.

The policeman had gone.

"It's just that…well, sir, tonight's the special exhibition, innit? The Mask of Mar…Marmoset the Third."

"*Mahamouset*," sighed Corneille. "You had the serious intention of a visit to the British Museum?"

"Yessir. The Mask of…Ma…*ha*…mou…set," he smiled as Corneille nodded his approval of the pronounciation, "well, it's the talk of the town, innit sir?"

Corneille nodded, thought. "I will make you this promise, Master Turner. If you assist me this night, I will grant you tomorrow afternoon to visit this exhibition most unique."

The boy nodded excitedly.

"I will, however, make one condition."

The boy arched one eyebrow in apprehension.

"You will take with you a block of paper and sketching pencils and you will make for me the representation most accurate of this fabled mask, yes?"

Turner smiled and nodded like a steam pump. "Oh yessir, yessir indeed I will."

ΨΨΨΨΨΨ

The Vienna clock struck twelve. Corneille stiffened. Ordinarily, the timepiece's rich, sonorous chime was a soothing sound, but…

He dabbed his mouth with the soft cotton handkerchief, folded the pink waxed tissue carefully over the remaining *chocolats noirs*, took himself to the window and looked at the array of artist's oils once again, their metal tubes tucked snugly into their rosewood rack. His verification was entirely superfluous. The transposition of Burnt Sienna and Raw Sienna on the second shelf was an affront to his colourman's eye, but it was the required signal in this instance. He longed to return the paints to their proper order but could not, not yet. His skin itched in discomfort.

Had the policeman noticed? Was a report noting the discontinuity of hues accelerating through the pneumatic tubes of Scotland Yard at this same moment? Was this blatant disarrangement in the perfect window of Louis Corneille et Fils already the subject of resolute analysis by the Police Engine? Was the infernal machine already directing a squad of officers to the armoury for immediate dispatch to this den of *trahison*?

He wondered for how much longer he could do this but knew with sad certainty that he would do it until his death. Unlike his father, also Louis, he had no *fils* to take over the reins when he passed. Murgatroyd would have done it, was being cultivated for the precise purpose indeed, but Murgatroyd's body had washed up on the banks of the Thames near the Colossus not six months prior, the pallid corpse caught by the goddess's unearthly beams as the fog began to roll in off the estuary. Murder by persons unknown, the coroner had adjudged. Corneille had presumed he would be next and had been on tenterhooks ever since.

The police had, of course, come to the shop to question Murgatroyd's employer and Corncille had let his genuine grief cover his panic. Had they known? Had the sharp-eyed detective seen through the charade? They had not returned to arrest him afterwards, although he had anticipated such an action for weeks after the incident. But then they were crafty, these English policemen. They watched, they waited, they struck at the very moment of best advantage, when the game was at its most dangerous.

And this was a dangerous, *dangerous* game.

An icy chill fluttered across his brow. Through the steam rising from his latest mug of *tisane*, his third of the day, he could see a figure at the window, studying the display. Corneille placed the mug carefully on the countertop and wiped the steam from his *pince-nez*. He replaced the spectacles quickly and was relieved to see this was not a policeman.

The entry bell tinkled as the man entered the shop. He looked around quickly to make sure nobody else was there and made straight for the counter.

Corneille shivered with recognition.

The gentleman was a queer-looking fellow, tall and angular of face. He wore a top hat of a striking Tempered Viridian velvet, wound with contrasting cord of Alzarin Crimson. His pale, sinewy neck stuck from an expensive gabardine coat with a neat fur collar in the Crimean style. He wore spectacles, the copper frame so light it seemed only to be made from wire, and the lenses dark, as an albino might rely upon. The man's gaunt face, pinched by the November streets, sported dabs of the palest Vermillion atop an English tan, gained no doubt in what they called the "English Riviera", Torquay or Bournemouth or somewhere equally hideous. No victim of albinism *this*.

When he spoke, it was with a distinctly suburban accent, undercut with a dark thread of menace. Or was that simply Corneille's imagination? "Do you have Cadmium Yellow?"

It was the correct response to the signal of the Siennas.

"In oil or watercolour?" Corneille's voice wavered slightly. He felt hot.

"Oh, oil of course." The man smiled toothily, one gold incisor flashing.

"Alas, monsieur, I do not have it right away, but I am able to obtain it in a matter of hours from my warehouse if that is acceptable?"

The man nodded. "At what time?"

"You may collect it at…" Corneille consulted the Vienna clock, "…*dix heures et demi*."

"That is somewhat *late*."

"Such a delicate hue requires…preparation."

"I see." The man turned on his heel. "Ten-thirty o'clock tonight then."

He left.

Turner emerged from the stockroom. "Blimey, he must be desperate to paint something yellow!"

"Yes," said Corneille, sipping his tisane. So, the lad had been listening. How very…*enterprising* of him. Corneille made his face a mask. "He is very keen to obtain his merchandise. I am going to close the shop early so that we two may be about our business."

ΨΨΨΨΨΨ

The circular stairway to the basement of Corneille et Fils was closed to the general public via the mechanism of a thick velvet rope in a striking Prussian Blue. The basement was a stockroom and a storeroom for a variety of artists, those who had no storage space in their garret in Borough or Camden but could scrape together a few shillings a month for their works to be stored and, on occasion, sold for commission by Louis Corneille. The boy Turner was, naturally, allowed into the sanctum to retrieve such items as might be required in the shop above, but was unaware of its true nature, of its *secret veritable*.

At the centre of the basement, under three powerful electric lights, sat a venerable workbench. Here Corneille would mix the small quantities of his custom paints and varnishes, but tonight was about combinations of a different register. He watched as the boy, directed by him, pulled casks and mason jars from the shelving around the room and placed each item carefully on the bench. Three squat drums the size of hat boxes stood open at one end. Three six-inch lengths of what looked like lacquered black cord and three metal discs the exact size of the diameter of the interior of each drum sat by their side.

"What's this then?" said Turner, his tone without suspicion or recrimination.

Corneille fixed him with his hardest stare. "It is an enterprise of the most delicate nature, Monsieur Turner. You have been a highly trustworthy *assistant*, and in this I have elected to trust you to the utmost. You will not speak of this. To your knowledge we are engaged in the mixture of the most rarefied colours. Do you understand?"

The boy nodded.

Corneille had considered paying him, but the problem with paying for silence was that the pay grew steadily higher and the possibility of outright blackmail raised its ugly head very quickly. Trust, trust was a rarer and more powerful currency by far. He looked at the boy intently, tipping his head gently to one side as if assaying Turner.

This had the desired effect. Turner flashed a tight smile. "Shall we get on with it then, Monsieur? If your gentleman in the green hat and glasses is arriving at ten thirty, we should be about our business, no?"

"Correct!" Corneille began to move around the workspace, having the boy unscrew some jars and uncork others for him while *il maestro* took from them a demiard of this, a peck of that, a salt spoon of another. Everything was weighed carefully on a brass scale and poured into a large stone mortar. While Corneille added further elements, the boy ground them into paste with the forearm-sized pestle. A faint odour of ammonium and linseed oil began to rise from their industry.

The boy watched, fascinated by his employer's purpose and precision, occasionally directed to pass this or that tub of gum, jar of varnish, flask of spirit. The final mixing took place in an old butter churn, such was the quantity of what Monsieur Corneille called *base*. As the boy mixed, Corneille busied himself with a sheet of mixing glass and a much smaller quantity of pigment and medium to create the Cadmium Yellow which would, finally, be layered upon the *base*. Turner looked puzzled but did not question.

A good quarter of an hour passed. Then, abruptly, Corneille adjudged the mixing to be *suffisant*, and had

Turner pour it into the three drums until each was nearly three-quarters full. He then placed an empty coffee can into the centre of the puffy white *base* in each drum, pushing it down until just half an inch of its cylindrical form was visible.

"Is that it then?" Turner wiped the sweat from his brow. It was warm in the basement and the boy had been hard at work.

Corneille's physical exertions had been trifling. He was sweating for a very different reason. "Not quite, no. There is one final component." This was the moment of truth, the greatest risk to the enterprise.

Murgatroyd, younger, fitter and almost fearless, certainly in comparison to Corneille, had completed this part of the task in times past. But Murgatroyd was dead, likely at the hands of the Imperial Secret Police, who did not exist of course. The Empire, officially, had no need of Dark Lanterns, yet everyone knew the truth of them and their 'secret' headquarters at Somerset House on the north side of Waterloo Bridge.

When Corneille employed Turner as Murgatroyd's replacement, he had surveilled the boy carefully, very carefully indeed, on one occasion even following him home to the dingy room in a sooty townhouse in Leyton where the young man resided. It had taken a full hour to walk back from Turner's digs to the Bow Road pneumatic railway station, ducking into dark alleyways to avoid thugs and the occasional harlot. For weeks afterwards Corneille watched the lad, but his fears seemed to be groundless. Turner seemed to have no interest in politics whatever, barely knew who any of the Cabinet were.

Aside from his unusual like for art, he seemed mainly to be concerned with beer, girls and the electric dogs. He had relatives, no apparent confidants. He was a boy of no account whatever.

"That's not the last of it then?" said Turner.

Corneille nodded towards a glass jug replete with a pale liquid. "Have your lemonade first. It will refresh and invigorate."

The lad poured himself a glass of the fresh lemonade and sucked it down greedily. "Righty-o, what's next then?"

Corneille stepped to the tall wooden cabinet which contained eighteen drawers. "This, my dear Monsieur Turner, is the very acme of the trust I spoke of before. Until now you have assisted me in the assembly of an unexceptional compound. If you wish to leave now, I will understand. But if you wish to take the next step, I will proceed."

Turner nodded without hesitation.

Corneille breathed out and pulled the drawer handle of the ninth drawer, twisting it exactly one quarter turn anticlockwise.

To the boy's clear amazement, the fake drawer fronts came away as a piece, swinging on well-oiled hinges to reveal a door. "Flippin' 'eck!"

"That is where we need to go next, I am afraid," said Corneille.

"Where does it go?"

"Behind that door is a stairwell. You will take this lamp and descend the staircase ahead of me but be *very* careful as you do. It will lead to the right as it descends and when you reach the *fond* you must halt. Ahead of you is another door, a metal one of precise curvature, with a brass handle. On *no account* are you to open this door immediately. Instead, you must listen."

"What am I listening for?"

"A train."

"A *train*?"

"*Précisement*."

The boy looked shocked.

"The curved door was a construction entrance for the pneumatic railway," continued Corneille. "You must wait until the train is passed and then open the door. You will descend into the tube and make your way to another identical door immediately opposite, taking the lamp so that you should not stumble on the recessed tracks. This door has a combination lock, rather like a bank vault, do you see? You will turn the dial left twenty clicks, right twelve clicks and left again ten, and the door will open. Behind the door is a small room, which was previously a storeroom. You will enter. You will see a number of small barrels. I want you to pick up one of the barrels with the white label and one with the yellow label, do you understand? I think a strong boy such as yourself may be able to manage both at the same time, but you may have to conduct two *sorties*."

"What is in the barrels?"

"It is of no importance."

Turner looked at him with a hurt expression. "I am your trusted assistant, you told me so yourself, Monsieur."

"Trust me," said Corneille. "In this case, ignorance is your security. The less you know about this enterprise the better it will be for you. So, are you clear? Two barrels, one with the label which is white, the other the label which is yellow. And most important of all, do *not* drop the barrels. And make *very* sure that you only cross the tunnel immediately after you hear a train pass."

"Yes, sir, Monsieur Corneille."

"Very good. I will descend to the second stair to assist you."

The boy began to make his way down. Corneille followed him and the swaying lamplight. In less than a minute, the boy had reached the bottom of the stairs, with Corneille two steps behind him.

Turner found the lamp-hook and hung his lamp on it, bathing the curved metal door in its amber light, which in turn illuminated the full extent of the brick cubby hole which provided access to the Edgmorden Line of London's Pneumatic Underground Railway.

"Wait, now." Corneille halted, lighting another lamp which hung at the bottom of the stairwell.

"Very good." Turner smiled, hawked and spat on the floor.

Corneille wrinkled his nose in faint disgust, but the boy did not see.

They waited. It was hotter down here and soon both of them were sweating copiously. Corneille, who had had an evening of varnish and gum in his nostrils now began to smell the boy, this infrequently washed London youngster, the sinew and fibre of the Empire, who would doubtless be wrenched from his comfortable position at Corneille et Fils to the trenches of the Crimea or the blasted wastes of the Transvaal at the first sign of war. He almost pitied him. But their task made no room for pity. This enterprise made no room for finer feeling of any kind. The stakes were just too high, the price of failure, deadly.

The door made a faint 'dink' noise as the pressure in the tunnel beyond increased. A train was coming. The walls began to vibrate slightly, the lamp swung a little on its hook. Then, at once, a fearsome, howling noise came on rapidly and cut off five seconds later. The whole room trembled, shuddered.

"Now!" said Corneille.

The boy looked around at him and slammed down the big brass handle. The door's rubber seal popped, and it swung inwards.

"Remember, left twenty, right twelve, left ten, then in. One white barrel, one yellow."

"Right-o," said Turner.

"And hurry!"

The boy disappeared, and Corneille made his way to the doorway, noting the swinging passage of the lamp which cast the boy's shadow around the curved, sloping, soot-streaked metal of the tunnel.

The smell of sweat and burned lamp oil was quickly overwhelmed by the stench of the Tube, a creeping, sizzling odour of burned rubber, rancid oil and stinking Thames water.

"Left twenty…" came the boy's voice.

"Right twelve, then left ten again." Corneille could hear the tremor in his own voice as he shouted the instructions. "Carefully! Or you will need to zero the dial and *recommence*."

A grunt came in response.

Corneille peered into the Tube. Turner had set the lamp down on the curved floor next to one of the inset tracks, where it wobbled slightly on the uneven angle of the tunnel in the descent from King's Cross towards Leicester Square. Murgatroyd had once lost a lamp. It had tipped and rolled away from him, down and down and down the tunnel until a train must have ground it to pieces. That had been a very nervous night, with Murgatroyd relying on his foreknowledge and keen sense of hearing to open the dial lock. He had succeeded less than half a minute before the Golders Green to Clapham Common train had barrelled through at a ferocious pace. Corneille had only just managed to secure his door, so frightened had he been, and they had uncorked a bottle of twenty-year-old Armagnac later, when they had done, so relieved was he to have the man back safe and sound.

Turner managed to open the door without issue and was soon safely inside. He emerged seconds later, placed the lamp on the lintel of the door, then reached back inside for the two small barrels, tucking one under each arm and started making his way carefully back across the curved tunnel.

Corneille watched the encumbered silhouette nervously. Around halfway across, it wobbled as a foot went out from under it. The shadow slammed to the floor of the tunnel and one of the barrels went rolling away down the tunnel.

"Shit!"

Corneille felt a cold trickle of sweat course down his spine and into his silk underwear. "Do not panic, Monsieur Turner! You have plenty of time. Retrieve another barrel and take exceptional care this time!"

The shadow had already made its way back to the far door and disappeared into the storeroom.

Corneille pulled out his pocket-watch and took his *pince-nez* from the other pocket of his waistcoat. He struggled to read the time, so shaky were his hands.

9.48.

The last train had passed at 9.44. Moving to Imperial Time, the trains were always punctual to the second. The next one would be along in two minutes. Plenty of time, he told himself. *Plenty of time.*

He looked back into the tunnel. The silhouette once again made its way across, more slowly, carefully this time, and in a matter of seconds, Turner's sweaty face swam into view in the doorway. He dumped first one and then the second barrel inside Corneille's door and began to clamber up.

"What are you doing?" hissed Corneille. "You must close the other door!"

Turner's eyes went wide, his ruddy face blanching. He said nothing, simply turned and began to clamber across the tunnel again.

Corneille moved each barrel inside with his foot. One tipped onto its side and rolled to the corner. Its yellow label was, of course, entirely blank. Even if the police did manage to retrieve the lost barrel – highly unlikely, for the current of air travelling ahead of the train would blast it along the platform gully at Leicester Square and into the next tunnel, if it had not been crushed already by the train itself – they would have no clue where it came from. Its contents would shed no further light. Of course, if the boy had dropped both barrels, then those unfortunate enough to be waiting on the platform at Leicester Square might be meeting a fiery doom, and the gig would be up, for sure.

Corneille peered into the tunnel. A gust of warm air brushed his right cheek.

No!

Corneille looked at his watch again. It was a fine time-piece, handed to him by his father on the old man's death-bed. Of late, though, it had begun to lose a few seconds here and there. He had been meaning to take it to Ossuary Row, to the Clockwork Clockmaker, but one became so busy at this time of year…

On the other side of the tunnel, Turner closed the door and Corneille could hear the locking mechanism spin. The boy picked the light up from the tunnel floor and a stray leaf danced through it like a drunken bat.

"Quickly!" Corneille began to perspire freely. The pressure of air on the right side of his face was growing steadily greater, cooling the sweat running down it.

The safety lamp bobbed as Turner ran, then abruptly dropped to one side with a clattering sound as it hit the tunnel floor. "Ow!"

"Get up! Quickly!"

The boy clambered up and stepped carefully over the track in front of him.

Corneille pulled out his pocket watch again.

9.49.

Corneille could hear the noise now, a deep thrumming undercut by a low rumbling sound. The tunnel was full of wind.

The boy looked up, his face stricken with panic, ghoul-ish as the lamplight took it from below.

Suddenly, Corneille was in the corner of the room, watching himself. He saw his hand go to the large brass handle and saw it push the door until it closed. The disembodied hand pushed the handle up to lock the door.

Only a boy...

Corneille dropped to the floor, back against the door. Distantly he was aware of moisture in his pants, though he knew not whether he had sat in a puddle or simply his own perspiration.

There was a thump as the boy hit the other side of the door, and a series of frantic, muffled cries of pure terror above more thumping.

Just a boy...

The Morden train barrelled through, right on the dot, a few inches of air and an inch of metal away from Corneille. He could feel every axle on every carriage as a judder in his back as the door flexed and groaned behind him.

In the train's wake, an eerie silence. The lamp fizzed malevolently, and Corneille was pulled away from the edge of his darkest thoughts.

His head was swimming, hands trembling. He picked up one of the barrels. He was not a young man, but the cask was not heavy, so he began the ascent, leaving the fizzing lamp on its hook. Beneath his shirt, his linen under-vest was soaked through. He had never felt more wretched. His legs felt like aspic, the barrel seemed weighted with lead. Step by step by step he climbed, until he altogether forgot he was in the brick stairwell underneath his shop. Instead, he imagined he was mounting an endless stairway which wound and wound and wound to infinity, growing steadily darker with each deep tread. The blackness enveloped him completely now. The barrel and he seemed joined together. Every muscle of his body ached, every sinew was drawn tight as catgut. When he closed his eyes, he could see the boy's face, a blur of Flake White, burnished with Yellow Ochre from the swaying lamplight.

Only a boy.

They are ten a penny.

Some sacrifices must be made for the Cause.

His heart fluttered in his chest. His clothes were sodden, clinging, as if he had become entangled in a line of wet sheets on a blustery day. He could taste ash and filth and salt and something metallic. His mouth was paste-dry. He wondered absently whether he might die here and fall down and down and down the circular stairwell into oblivion.

Then, suddenly, it was over. He had reached the door to the basement.

He opened it with what seemed like his last scrap of strength, and half-lowered, half-dropped the barrel to the floor before joining it himself. He stayed there, on hands and knees, for some time, trying to catch his breath. Cold sweat flowed from head, armpits, groin and pooled in the ditch of his spine. He wondered if he would vomit but the feeling passed, and he struggled to his feet. The half-full jug of lemonade glinted tantalisingly on the workbench, the boy's glass sat beside it.

Only a boy.

Corneille poured himself a glass and took half of it in one long gulp, feeling some of it spill over his bottom lip down the front of his sweat-marked shirt and damp waistcoat.

He raised the glass up to the level of his face.

Cadmium Yellow Light. Flake White. Ochre. And a hint of Cerulean Blue, for the tinge of green in this restorative elixir.

He picked up the battered moleskin notebook he usually carried from the edge of the bench where he had left it before the descent, found the page marked 'L' and made a note of the combination, then drank the rest of the glass down.

Somewhat fortified, he made for the door to the basement to retrieve the second barrel. It was then that he noticed the boy's canvas satchel on the floor by the workbench.

He glanced once again at his pocket watch.

10.05.

Should be 10.06.

The strange gaunt-faced gentleman in the Tempered Viridian hat and ridiculous spectacles may already be here. He could be in the shop, waiting impatiently.

Everything was in order.

Sacrifices had been made.

For the Cause.

One faded leather strap had come undone and out of the bag peeked the corner of a sketchbook. Corneille bent to pick up the satchel and placed it on the bench, drawing out the book as he did so. It was a fine book with a black leather cover and beautiful ivory sketching vellum, one of Corneille's own that the boy had purchased from the shop with his first week's salary and the benefit of staff discount.

Corneille opened it. On the first page was a highly

detailed depiction of the statue of Anteros in Piccadilly Circus. The boy's pencilwork was exceptional, though the shakily inked title showed his mastery of calligraphy was not its equal. On the next page was the Colossus of the Thames, viewed from the Outer Docks, looming impressionistically through a suggestive fog bank. Then the Houses of Parliament in all their Gothic glory. Then the Armamentarium at Smithfield, the hated source of all the Empire's *malaise*.

The next page was blank except for a painstakingly inked name: Mahamouset.

A drop of water fell onto the 'h' and rolled down the smooth paper, leaving a shiny wake of Prussian Blue and Dark Violet and a tail of Payne's Grey.

At first Corneille thought the water was a bead of sweat from his brow.

But then more tears came, erasing the exalted pharaoh in a welter of splashes and streaks of deadly colour.

ΨΨΨΨΨΨ

ᴛʜᴇ LOST POETS

"BEAUMONT, BOWES, CAMPBELL, Chaucer, Davenant, Denham, Drayton, Dryden, Gay, Gifford, Macaulay, Macpherson, Prior, Rowe, Sheridan, South, Spenser…" The old man's Sussex drawl echoed from the stone walls in this corner of the Abbey. He tapped his briar pipe out on the wall and shuffled the loosened ash and dottle into the grate with his velveteen slipper. "Them's the bones, well, all that'll be left of them after the worms have done their work." He paused. "I'm meaning to say they're buried here under us, many of our finest poets, or my name's not Edward Jones."

The lad looked bored, but Jones pressed on regardless. "Look around you and you'll see the other denizens. In name, if not bone."

The lad looked around him, up and down, at the various statues and tablets, clearly not taking anything in. He yawned and picked at something stuck in his teeth.

Jones tutted and rapped his pipe on the marble tablet next to him.

The boy was plucked from his indifference, at least momentarily. "Sorry, grandad."

Jones nodded. "Ah well, I was a lad once too. Allow me to illuminate. That statue's Addison, the tablet yonder is

Anstey. Then Samuel Butler, there, see? And Goldsmith, Gray, and that new bust there is Keble. Then Mason, Milton, Philips and then, the master of them all, if you'll be asking my opinion on the matter, William Wordsworth, our most recent Laureate." He cleared his throat. "I wandered lonely as a..." He gestured for the lad to complete the line.

"Clown?"

"Clown?" echoed Jones. "*Clown*? Since when have clowns been lonely? They've a whole circus to keep 'em company!" He went to clip the lad's ear, but the boy moved out of range, anticipating the censure. "Clowns, my life," he muttered, and began refilling his pipe.

"I still don't get why I 'ave to learn all this stuff."

The lad's London drawl was quite pronounced now, doubtless something of an affection he'd picked up at school, to fit in. It was good Sussex they spoke at home, the soft, open talk of the Downs, but such a rustic mode would attract bullies, Jones reasoned.

How best to handle this? He narrowed his eyes so much they disappeared under his bushy brows. "Because, lad, it's important knowledge. And knowledge is power. And someone's got to know it. And because I promised your grandmother I wouldn't let you grow up without knowing all I could tell you about literature and the arts. Oh, I know it's all about engineering and steam and ruddy airships and pneumatic railways these days, that's all you lads seem interested in. But art is what stirs the soul."

The lad harrumphed. "So when I am gonna learn about the Lost Poets?"

Jones coughed loudly, practically dropped his pipe. "Shhhhh! Guard your tongue!"

"What? I only said…"

"I know what you 'only said'. And you can button it back up in your head, while you're in here. You don't talk of the Lost Ones while you're in the company of these fine spirits. That's for another time."

The lad looked disconsolate.

Jones' heart thawed in the heat of his grandson's disappointment. "Let's go for a walk on the Green. I could do with getting a little fresh air."

The lad dug his hands into his pockets and adopted his deepest pout.

Jones looked at him. Had he been any different when he was a lad, before that fateful day? He supposed not. He felt in his waistcoat pocket and pulled out a white paper bag with a hard, congealed mass in it. "'Here, have a butterscotch."

The lad smiled broadly and took the bag from him, breaking off a sweet, creamy lump of Heaven.

ΨΨΨΨΨΨ

College Green was not busy at this time of day. Parliament was in session, and all the Members were in the House along with the close servants and reporters as might be found on the square stretch of lawn and pathways at other times.

Jones rummaged around in his pockets for a match. Then came the satisfying rasp of matchhead on sandpaper, and he set about sucking the tiny flame gently into the bowl of the pipe. He sat down next to the lad on one of the fine wrought iron benches. From above them came a rhythmic chugging sound, and their part of the Green fell into shadow.

All the better, he thought.

"Look, it's *The Queen Mary!*" The lad pointed to the gargantuan dirigible moving slowly through the thin smog a couple of hundred feet above.

"Not at this time, no lad, it'll be the *Hotspur*. See those bomb racks and the cupola for the Julien guns on the rear of the gondola? And the whole envelope is Navy Blue, the *Mary* is grey."

The lad shivered with awe. "Fearsome thing, eh Grandad?"

Jones made to ignore the flying contraption. "So..." He lowered his voice even though there was not a soul within a hundred feet of them and despite the thrum of the *Hotspur's* four propeller-engines. "You wanted to know about the Lost Poets. Well, that's a tale and a half I'll tell you, but we've not got long so I'll tell you the short version and you can make up your own mind, eh?"

The lad nodded.

"The Lost Poets is the name for the poets who fell out of favour with government. You remember those blank tablets and faceless busts in the Abbey around Poets' Corner?"

The lad nodded again, his attention piqued by the hint of rebellion.

"That was them. Until they got *erased*. The Blues went the length and breadth of Charing Cross Road collecting all the copies of all their books, and then had a big old bonfire in Cambridge Circus, right so's everyone could see. Then the Chief Constable his very self declared there and then that anyone found in possession of a copy of any of the outlawed poetry or even a page of it would be slung in jail, or maybe in *Bedlam*."

"Bedlam?" The lad's face was white as tapioca pudding.

"Aye," said Jones, puffing out a satisfying cloud of dense white smoke. "And that proper put the wind up all the booksellers, I tell you. From Camden Market to Spitalfields, the word went out, and there were burnings a'plenty." He felt a tear come to his eye.

"What happened then?"

"I'm getting to that. Well, nothing's so good at creating an interest as when the government tries to ban it. And so very soon, Radicals were scooping up any remaining copies of the Poets' work all over the country. Of course, folks out in the country take this sort of thing very seriously indeed and are mightily loyal to the Crown, so all the major cities had already hidden all theirs, if they could. There was a Radical bookshop in Manchester, which managed to smuggle some out, and some went to Glasgow, I believe. But the police were pretty thorough. Only one place they didn't dare touch."

"Where's that?"

"Ah, well, that *would* be telling now wouldn't it?"

"Aw no," said the lad. "You can't say that, not after givin' me all the build up!"

Edward Jones laughed softly and sucked on his pipe, then winced.

"Are you alright, grandad?"

Jones waved the concern away. "Ah, just my old arthritis. All those wet days sitting in fields, painting. Your grandmother warned me, but I was a stubborn man."

"So…you were telling me about some place where the Lost Poets are?"

Above them, the airship had almost passed, things threatened to return to normal. Jones bent his head towards his grandson in conspiratorial fashion. "Well, it's said that in Oxford, part of the University there, is a grand library what has all the books ever written."

"Ever?"

"Ever. It's a huge place with a big dome on top, but it goes miles under the Earth, brick cellars as long as Westminster Abbey itself, and corridors which would stretch from here to Piccadilly, with its own pneumatic trains to get the librarians from one end to the other. In those cellars are stored *everything*. And the librarians would sooner die than burn a single page of it, so it's said. Anyways, Oxford's where the Prime Ministers and bishops and 'alf the Bar comes from, so that Library is protected. And so, then, are the Lost Poets."

The lad nodded, wide-eyed.

"I s'pose there might be a copy of one of them here or there, hiding in some antiquarian in Stepney or in a gloomy cellar off Tottenham Court Road, but the Bodlean in Oxford has them all." He formed an 'O' with his mouth and blew a series of smoke rings into the air, to the lad's clear wonderment. "*All* of them."

"And *who* were they?" The lad practically whispered this time, reverent, *cautious*.

"Ah, I don't know all their names," said his grandfather, quietly. "The Librarians obviously do, and I daresay you might find a Radical you could get very drunk who might tell you. But the way I heard tell, they're nameless, for the most part.

Or at any rate you wouldn't want to get caught whispering one of their names, lest the coppers take you for a Radical."

"And why did the government ban them all and burn the books and threaten…*Bedlam*…?" asked the lad, his voice dropping to a whisper.

Jones lowered his voice. "It's said the Lost Poets are *dangerous*."

"Dangerous? How?"

"I am not rightly sure, to tell truth, lad." He cocked one eye and surveyed the Green for any eavesdroppers or, worse, coppers. "But it's said their verses could topple the government, bring down the Empire even."

The lad looked horrified. "Say it ain't so…"

"I don't know, lad. But it's best it remains a secret, eh?"

"When did all this happen?"

"Not long after Shelley died."

"Who?"

"Percy Bysshe Shelley," said Jones. "A fine poet, but a right radical, he was. Shelley smuggled some dark verses into collections of his, and others, Keats and Byron and the like." He winced, having promised himself he would never utter these names aloud.

"Keats? Byron?"

"Both very fine poets, you'll never have heard of them of course. Erased, along with Shelley." He drew his hand across his throat.

"That's what happened to them?"

"*Damnatio memoriae*," said Jones gravely. "Erased from history. Cancelled. Like they never existed."

"But you knew them? Were you there, then, at the burnings, grandad?"

"Ah." He blew a conical stream of smoke from the side of his mouth. He felt the tears again, burning hotly behind his eyes, threatening to escape. "I was young, just as you are now, but I remember it as clear as day. A huge pyre in Cambridge Circus, police everywhere, women crying, dogs howling and the whinnying of frightened horses. Terrible. It was a warm summer night and the flames got so great the hot air was pushing burning pages high into the sky."

"Pages?"

"Yes." Jones fixed his grandson with pale, rheumy eyes, reached inside his worn green jacket and pulled out a small piece of paper, burned along two edges and yellow with age.

"Is that…?"

"I found it in Cranbourne Street, on my way home. Pushed it into my pocket before anyone saw me."

"Is it one of…Miss Shelley's?"

"*Bysshe* Shelley. I have no idea. There's no author's name, just a couple of lines in some funny-looking type."

"What does it say?"

In the distance, they could still see the dark bulk of the *Hotspur*, prickling with guns, as it passed over the south end of Westminster Bridge, though its engines were naught but a low buzz now. It felt like the eye of government was off them, though they sat not two hundred yards from the Mother of All Parliaments herself.

This fact took the old Radical as ironic. His bones felt old. He had little life left in him. Perhaps the verse would galvanise the lad as it had him, all those years ago, inspire him to connect with the Radical movement, seek out allies and knowledge of the Lost Poets as he himself had done. Perhaps one day the lad would even get to don the white felt gloves and travel along the miniature pneumatic railway under the Bodlean, to take in the glory of the forbidden verse, as he had done.

Maybe he would tell the boy all that, before he went.

He handed the paper to the lad. "Here, take it."

The lad looked at the scrap as if it were gold. "Are you sure?"

"I'm an old man, I want you to have it. But don't go telling nobody about it. Guard it with your life, you hear me?"

The boy looked awestruck. He huddled in his coat and opened the folded fragment, and read it slowly, softly, away from any prying eyes.

"In his house at R'lyeh, dead Cthulhu lies dreaming..."

ΨΨΨΨΨΨ

The Button Man

"C'mon lass, you know the rules, I'm going to have to move you along."

Millie looked up at the beadle, a giant of a man with great rolling whiskers and a moustache like a Turk. Flakes of snow sparkled here and there on his dark frock coat and black top hat. His voice was kindly, but Millie could sense his tone belied his role – making sure the ladies and gents who frequented the Burlington Arcade could do so freely without having to navigate urchins, hawkers, ne'er-do-wells and little button-sellers like her.

She held out her hand, palm upwards. Sitting on it was the thick brass button she had been keeping for this very moment. It was a handsome thing, a plain dome inscribed with a rose, spun around with miniature rope, self-shanked in brass. That was rare. Cheaper makers might use tin or steel for the button-back and fastener, but this was a craftsman's button with MADE IN BRITAIN and a tiny Union flag hand-stamped next to the shank.

"What's that you've got there?" The beadle peered into her hand.

Millie used her other hand to point to the bottom-most button – or the space where it should be – on his coat. Her arm ached with the weight of the canvas bag slung over her shoulder, the bag which held all she owned, including the hundreds of buttons she hawked, all neatly affixed to strips of canvas-backed baize.

"Is that my button?" His voice held no hint of accusation, merely enquiry. "Where did you find that?"

She held up her hand to him, nodding for him to take the button. His big hand came down on hers and he took up the item, inspecting it carefully with his soft pale brown eyes. He pursed his lips under his fine moustache and put his hand around her shoulder.

"Can you sew?" The question was unnecessary. All girls could sew.

She nodded.

"Well, I'm going to need someone to fix this situation for me for sure!" He looked around and motioned to one of the other beadles. "Jim, this young lady has found my lost button. Its disappearance has vexed me for a few days on account of not wanting His Grace to see me in disarray. Could you watch this end while I take my little seamstress here to the office and have her mend it?"

The other man nodded, smiled lasciviously, as if these office trips were something of a regular event. She smiled nervously.

The beadle took her by the shoulder and motioned her into the Arcade. She had peered in from the entryway plenty of times, of course, but it was one thing being on the outside and quite another in the interior. Her eyes did not know where to look first, and soon she found her head swivelling to one marvel after another: pearl drop earrings, silver necklaces, crystal bottles of perfume the size of whisky decanters, fob watches like enormous gold buttons, clockwork automata which could pour your tea, hatpins and tiepins and antique dressers and tables and ornate gas lamps and plant stands and vases of lustrous Venetian glass.

And everywhere, lights. Globes of light above, electrical lights above every doorway and in the interior of every shop, and the lights of Christmas to boot. The casements of almost every window were festooned with tiny, impossible strings of lights on trees and statuettes and around, like a blizzard of stars.

The Burlington Arcade's famous Christmas lights were "butter upon bacon", as Mabel would have said, for the Arcade was a glittering jewel all by itself, but still the lights took Millie's breath away. She paused several times to look more closely at something here or there, and the beadle let her, for there were few customers on this dark December night, longest of the year.

"The hallway to Heaven itself couldn't look prettier," she said quietly.

The beadle smiled, guided her by the shoulder further along the glass-covered parade of shops.

Millie felt her hands beginning to ache as they slowly thawed. She realised that she couldn't remember the last time they had been properly warm.

"Come along, it's just through here." The beadle conducted her down a slim passageway between a fancy milliner's shop and an antiquarian bookseller, towards a smart black door. He opened it and motioned her into the Beadles' Office.

The office was a snug, windowless room with a second door to who-knew-where. The floor was worn boards, partly covered by a motley selection of threadbare rugs. A fire burned in the grate but there was a stove for good measure, with a tall metal jug upon it. A table, hosting a card game in progress with battered enamelled tin mugs by the suspended hands, four chairs and two worn armchairs, one either side of the fire with a low table between them, completed the furniture. The walls held two electrical wall lamps, a framed daguerreotype portrait of Her Imperial Majesty Alexandrina The Forever Queen, naturally, and a few shelves containing books and other paraphernalia, though judging by the faint cobwebs which adorned them, most had not been used of late.

Millie took in a huge breath of coffee and old pipe-smoke and warm carpet, a heavenly cocktail which almost made her forget her nerves.

Almost.

The beadle took his coat off and bade her sit in one of the armchairs. The warmth of the room was bliss, the feel of scuffed velvet below her hands most luxurious.

"Can't have you trying to sew with cold hands." He moved to the stove, returning with a steaming tin mug of black liquid. "Drink this."

"What is it?"

He laughed. "Coffee."

"Oh. I've never had it before."

"Be careful now, it's hot."

She sipped experimentally at it. It was hot, hotter than a pavement in July and bitter as an old maid's diary. "It's… good," she lied.

"Where are my manners?" said the beadle, fetching a grimy tin from one of the shelves. He dipped a stained teaspoon into it and retrieved a spoonful of a shiny substance the colour of ivory and the consistency of molasses. He dunked it into her coffee and stirred. Presently, the coffee turned a dark caramel colour. "Try it now."

"What is that stuff?"

"Sweetened condensed milk."

"It's...wondrous. I've never tasted anything like this."

"So, what's your name, girl." He sat down in the other armchair, looking even bigger out of his coat in his white shirt, fat blue tie and blue waistcoat. Silver shone in the crook of each elbow, where he wore a kind of bracelet of tight links which kept his sleeves in place.

"This is nice." She sipped at her sweet coffee.

He seemed unconcerned at her evasion. "And where do you find your buttons?"

She froze at the question, took a moment to answer. "People lose buttons all the time. I search the streets after dark, in gutters and sometimes in grates and down drains, if it's not raining. Course, you have to be careful."

"Careful?"

"That the Button Man don't get you."

"The Button Man?"

She put down her tin mug on the small table between them. "Needle and thread?"

He seemed to freeze, then regain himself. "Oh, yes..." He rose from his chair and moved to the far shelves above the table, rooted around for a moment. He brought back an old embroidered sewing pouch, placing it on the small table. "So, you were saying, the Button Man?"

"This is his time of year, the Button Man, when it's dark at four and when it's cold and wet, so's there's not as many people out in the street. The Button Man comes and takes you, takes what he reckons is his and you're never seen again."

"And where did you hear about this...Button Man?" There was a smile in his voice. She looked across at him. His soft eyes shone gold with captured firelight.

"All us girls know about the Button Man." Mille drew the sewing pouch to her. "If you're not careful, if you're alone, reaching for a shiny button in a drain or along an alleyway where there's nobody, he can take you then."

"Ah," said the beadle, as if he didn't believe a word of it.

"You don't believe me."

"And what does he want, this Button Man?" He pursed his lips in a wry smile which caused one side of his moustache to rise up his face. "What does he 'reckon is his'? Do you know?"

She sipped at her coffee. "Did you want me to sew your button on? My hands are warm now."

"We'll get to that. I want to hear more of this Button Man."

"It's said he collects lost buttons," she said, carefully.

"Lost buttons?" The beadle's eyes shone like a tiger's. "Fascinating."

"It's said the Button Man thinks all lost buttons belong to him, that each one is a charm to be used against its careless owner. If you've ever lost a button, you're fair game. And us girls, we lose plenty. Find 'em too of course. That's what makes him come for us 'specially."

The beadle laughed, an unexpectedly high sound from such a big man. "Oh, Millie, you do make me laugh."

She put down her empty mug on the little side table

next to the armchair and gripped the poker she had taken from the fireplace when he had risen to retrieve the sewing pouch. "I never told you my name."

The beadle looked at her, surprised. "Oh, *surely* you did." There was the faintest hint of something else in his velvet voice, a filigree of darkness.

She looked at him intently.

His eyes were brass buttons, gathering all the colours of flame from the fireplace into them. He smiled at her, eyebrows lifting, eyes widening. One of his eyes seemed to wobble and he flicked his eyebrow downwards as if trying to steady it.

Abruptly, it popped off, hit the top of his waistcoat by his collar bone, rolled down his front, bounced off the top of his right leg and onto the floor, then rolled over to Millie's chair, finally landing on its face, shank upwards. The void it had left in his face stared at her.

She bent to pick it up with her right hand. "Seems like you lost something." Her left hand gripped the poker tightly.

The Button Man opened his mouth to speak, but there came only a rattling sound, as if a whole box of buttons, lead, brass, bone, wood, glass, enamel, zinc, were being stirred slowly about.

Neither of them moved.

"Do you want me to sew it back on then?" She sat forward and dropped the poker onto the carpet.

He nodded slowly.

"I am a button-girl, after all," she said, reaching for the sewing pouch.

ѰѰѰѰѰѰ

ANTEBELLUM

"THIS, SIR, IS an affront to the dignity of the working man!"

The accusation rang out around the chamber. It was a packed house, and the heat was stifling. Lord knew, the summers in Her Imperial Majesty's Commonwealth of Kentucky could have horses fainting in the street and ladies taking to their beds, but it was one thing to be out in the fresh air, where one could seek shelter on a porch or underneath a hickory tree, and quite another to have to play sardines in the Senate chamber during a public hearing.

Donovan closed his eyes, feeling a rogue bead of sweat navigate its way across his eyebrow, fall and wriggle over the ridges of his eyelid, attacking his eye with its salty sting. Why had he not taken the Lieutenant Governorship of Connecticut when it had been offered to him? At least the Senate Chamber of the Nutmeg State had the latest Faraday Company steam-powered evaporative cooling system… Kentuckians, rather, seemed rather to take a perverse delight in the rejection of the technologic miracles which had made the Fifteen Colonies 'The Jewel of The Americas'.

Mary patted his hand. She was perspiring heavily, poor dear, her hair a little bedraggled, her damp lace collar chafing her lily-white swan's neck. She remained, nevertheless, quite the most beautiful woman he had ever seen.

Donovan was itching to say something in response to State Senator McConnell Fishwick Montgomery III, but the old blowhard in the white linen frockcoat and wide-brimmed hat had talked for nearly thirty minutes with scarcely a breath's pause, and at least six other senators had demonstrated an interest in adding their two pen'orth.

"These…*heathens*…" Montgomery jabbed one wrinkled claw at Donovan and his companion, "…aim to take the bread from the mouths of hardworking men, that they may starve in a ditch!" There was a hushed muttering from the chamber. Pressing his advantage, he continued to bluster. "They care nothing for the plight of the men tolling in the fields in the warmth of the sun Our Lord God Almighty created so that life may prosper. Life! Yes, I say again, life! Men working with their hands, not machines which assail the very earth with talons of brass and rods of steel, whose iron-shod wheels might crush a poor child's hand as easily as I might destroy a ripe plum." He pinched the invisible plum until its flesh split out of its skin. Somewhere in the upper gallery, a woman gasped.

"Their magnificent *devices*…" Montgomery sneered, pausing for effect, "…are manifestly the tools of the *Fallen One*, whose name shall never pass my lips in this hallowed arena."

The crowd murmured. A woman fainted in the gallery, whether from the heat or the hint of devilry it was impossible to tell. Several ladies around her gasped, and a hush came upon the chamber. All eyes went to the gallery as the lady in question, clad in a highly fashionable – yet highly inappropriate, given the heat – green French merino ensemble with matching hat, was manhandled to the exit. By the time she reached the open stairwell, she had regained a measure of wakefulness, yet still two young gentlemen felt it necessary to escort her to the relative cool of the peach orchard which lay behind the State House.

Montgomery paused as she made her exit, holding his wide-brimmed hat to his chest as if she had died rather than merely passed out. "As I was saying, these *devices…*"

"Time." The Speaker tapped his gavel on its rosewood block. The crowd murmured its dissent. A few men stamped their feet, clearly attempting to encourage a widespread reaction, but none was forthcoming – it was too hot for shenanigans – and the noise quickly faded.

Montgomery seethed, fists clenching involuntarily. He took a step back as if hit by some invisible force, then regained his composure and made a sarcastic half-bow, sweeping one white jacketed arm from left to right in a dramatic gesture of yielding the floor.

His Republican opponent stood up. There were a few hisses from the crowd, which the Speaker quickly quieted. State Senator Jackson De'Ath, dressed in a conservative Yankee suit and matching dark necktie, his pale face pinched beneath his bald pate, smiled tightly at the Speaker and nodded towards Donovan. "I yield my time to our special witness Doctor Donovan." He sat down amid his small clique of like-minded colleagues, who all nodded and congratulated him. This was the part they had all been waiting for.

The crowd knew it too. There came more hisses, louder this time. A balled-up order paper arced from the gallery and bounced twice to land at Donovan's feet as he stood up. There were sniggers from the gallery. Montgomery's expression had changed to one of quiet satisfaction. This was, after all, his home turf.

The Speaker looked up sharply. "If members of the public are unable to restrain themselves from discourtesy, they should be cognisant of the fact that I possess the ultimate authority to dissolve this assembly and to institute in its place a closed session of the State Senate."

That's House Speaker Jeffries, thought Donovan, *why use two words when you could use ten?* But he was grateful for the support, which he hadn't always had on this seemingly interminable tour. He moved to the lectern and tapped his papers on it, settling them and his nerves. He looked at the block of puffed-up Democrat state senators seated behind Montgomery, with their expensive white linen suits, thin ties and preposterous hats, and then to the crowd in the floor seats and tiered gallery. It was without doubt *their* crowd, riled up by the heat and the spectre of change.

He cleared his throat. "Mr Speaker, distinguished senators, gentlemen and ladies of Kentucky…"

He saw a few jiggling handkerchiefs and a scattering of waved order papers in the public gallery. Donovan was a handsome man, and his appearance had been the talk of the more refined Lexington *salons* for nearly a week now. A few disgruntled murmurs caused the wayward females, clearly desirous of the young doctor's attention, to withdraw their lace tokens, but the waving of the order papers indicated the crowd was not uniformly hostile. He felt his heart swell and a tear prick his eye. It was enough, this indication of modest support for the inevitable.

"For several decades now, some of you have witnessed the power of steam engines on your plantations. A few of you have installed steam threshing machines, horse rakers and reapers. A few more of you have engaged machines on deep plowing or the digging of drainage ditches. Steam power is known among you and rightly appreciated by you."

He paused then, to allow them to reflect on how these innovations had improved their lives, though casting his gaze around he could only see sceptical faces. "I am here to introduce you to the next stage of our Technical Revolution."

The crowd murmured. The word 'revolution' was freighted with riot, looting, chaos, mostly inspired by daguerrotypes of the Fall of the Manhattan Commune. He immediately regretted using it – he had thought he had excised the word from his presentation, but there it was, back again like a bad penny.

"And when I say 'revolution', of course I mean Progress."

Mary glared at him. The word 'progress' was almost as bad for conservative farming folk. She shook her head rapidly twice to the right, as if to say *move on now!*

He tried to do just that. "Many of you, I know, have concerns about the new Deere & Company harvest engines, but let me reassure you, gentlemen, there is nothing to fear. Far from it. The new machines will be a boon beyond your wildest expectations. It is not simply my firm belief but is supported by the evidence we have to date, that these fine machines will maximise the yield of every plantation in Kentucky, whether it be cotton or tobacco or hemp. The Deere Precision Harvester, for example, is sophisticated enough to pick peaches from the trees without leaving a single bruise upon them."

There were murmurs. Was he cutting through?

"I have recently come from Bordeaux, Mississippi, the site of one of the most significant investments in these new Deere machines. I can confirm that Bordeaux saw an almost *fifteen per cent* increase in crop yields during the first year of operation." He paused again. More murmurs, clearly questioning, some even intrigued, he thought.

"Frenchie lies!" came a shout from the gallery, accompanied by an outbreak of hooting and jeering.

Donovan knew better than to leave the jibe unchallenged, lest it propagate more unrest. He held up the papers, addressing himself to the place where he fancied the naysayer sat. "I have here in my hand a survey report conducted by the Royal Commission on Agriculture on behalf of Her Imperial Majesty Alexandrina, the Forever Queen."

The royal reference quieted the crowd. Kentuckians were fiercely loyal to the Crown and proud to be part of the Empire. For some indeed, Monarchy was next to Godliness. If the Queen endorsed something, they would follow, surely.

Donovan continued. "This is not French data, but British, approved by the most senior ministers of the Crown and every relevant scientist in the Royal Society. The Commission found quite clearly that in addition to improving yields across virtually all product groups, there was a significant improvement in the…" he paused. This was the most contentious part of his presentation. He had practised this material in detail but had found that in this part of the Fifteen Colonies, the message had an unpleasant taste. From Boston to Richmond, his machines had been marvelled at. But he'd faced hostility in Charleston, and there had almost been a riot in Savannah.

He regained his thrust. "A significant improvement, as I say, in the living conditions of those previously… *engaged* to work the land, as they were redeployed under, er, improved contracts."

Montgomery jumped to his feet and motioned to the Speaker. The Speaker coughed and Donovan could do nothing but yield, temporarily.

"Let us not beat about the bush," said Montgomery, his voice laced with menace. "The people of the great Commonwealth of Kentucky are not stupid, Mr Donovan. They see exactly what you mean when you talk of *improved contracts* and *redeployment*." He spat the words, using two fingers of each hand to affect quote marks in the London style to ram home the point. "You mean to take men off the land and replace them with *machines*!"

Donovan met the point head on. "That is the general idea, yes."

More gasps from the crowd. Montgomery let an alligator smile bisect his face.

Donovan looked at Mary who flashed him a tight smile under a determined frown, encouraging him to hold his nerve and press on. These people *had* to bow to the reality of progress. The Deere engines were the very spearpoint of that reality.

"You do understand what this *means*?" said Montgomery, more to the crowd than Donovan. He knew precisely what it meant, even if some of his constituents had not managed to puzzle it out yet.

Donovan held firm. "Fully. Men will be free to pursue gainful employment as they *choose*. They will become full members of society, with all the rights – "

"Do you hear this?" shouted Montgomery to the rafters. "These people wish to emancipate the working man! You, Mr Donovan, do not understand. These men are *property*. They are *our* property. You have no right to take them away."

"They are *people*," said Donovan, firmly.

"They are *negroes*," said Montgomery, letting the word roll off his tongue like a poisonous pebble.

"You can free them and be better off," said Donovan. "It has been shown time and again that machines work better than men in the course of the most laborious activities!" He felt his anger building now. He had tried to restrain himself, but on the subject of the greatest injustice man could visit upon another man, his passions rose, and ofttimes led him down a troublesome path.

Senator De'Ath nodded in approval, but the crowd was against both of them. Crumpled order papers began raining down from the gallery.

The Speaker banged his gavel repeatedly, bidding Donovan and Montgomery to be seated. "This will cease immediately, or I will order that this become a Closed Session! I will have the marshals arrest anyone who breaches this decree, under the charge of Contempt of Congress!"

The projectiles stopped, as did the shouting, but there

was an undercurrent of dissent and, at its borders, shock. The crowd now saw the full implications of the Deere machines: to turn Kentuckian society on its head.

"So, you admit this, Mr Donovan." Montgomery was on his feet again. The Speaker allowed him to infringe on De'Ath's time, seemingly preferring orderly conduct in the chamber to actual debate. "That your agenda is full emancipation of the negro?"

Donovan stood. "If you mean the *transformation* of the negro from a fearful, inefficient tool, with a short lifespan which can be summarily shortened by the cruelty of his owner, into a productive, long-lived member of society and rightful consumer of produced goods and a property-owner in his own right, a free man in our great country of opportunity, why then yes, I do freely admit this."

The crowd reeled in stunned silence.

"I rest my case," said Montgomery, bringing the entire weight of his training at the Kentuckian Bar to bear. "This is not about *machines*. It is not about *productivity*. It is about elevating the negro, against the specific injunctions of the Holy Bible, to equal status with landowners and their kin. It is about taking what is ours and distributing it in the manner of the Communards, elevating the negro to parity with *us*."

The crowd drew in a collective breath.

"These machines can pick cotton more effectively than any negro," snapped Donovan. "There is no need for slavery, not any longer. This barbarism no longer persists in any other corner of the Empire. The Federal Government, backed by the Crown, is providing seed capital for investment, interest free loans for the purchase of the Deere harvest machines by any farmer who cedes his right to own slaves and who liberates his 'working men' so that they might be free."

Montgomery spat on the floor, for real this time. "This cannot *stand*."

"Senator," said Donovan tersely. "This is the way of the future. Negro lives *matter*."

"Sir." Montgomery took up his silver-topped cane and shook it defiantly at Donovan. "This is a future which will be reached only *over my dead body* and the dead bodies of every proud son of Kentucky, and in the disdainful eye of our wrathful Lord."

Senator De'Ath hung his head, shook it sadly from side to side.

Donovan sat down. He felt his head drop. There were a hundred Montgomerys in the state senates, tens of thousands of men who would bring faith into any argument, the ultimate bulwark against the tide of progress.

Mary took his hand, patted it.

Donovan raised his head to look at her, this paragon of loyalty, his fierce defender, his love.

He looked at Montgomery, whose eyes were fixed on Mary's hand. He saw the senator's lip curl under the long, curved moustache, saw him mouth the word 'harlot' then gaze at Donovan with an expression of self-satisfaction, of victory.

It had been inevitable this moment, the greatest minds in Washington D.C. had opined when they sanctioned this expedition. They were ready for it. Some welcomed it.

He, Seamus Donovan, had lit the spark of war, and though he was confident Right would prevail, he wondered how many people would die before the scourge of slavery was banished from the land and the Age of the Machine could begin in earnest.

ΨΨΨΨΨΨ

The FOREVER QUEEN

"BUT...BUT..." THE TAILOR was red in the face, clearly flustered. It might be the heat of this latest oppressive London summer. It might be the weight of the swags of fabric he had been forced to carry up the long, broad flight of stairs in the entryway to the Palace. Or it might be frustration at the abrupt cancellation of his long-awaited appointment with Her Royal Highness Alexandrina, Empress of India, the Good Hope and the Fifteen Colonies.

It could, conceivably, be all three. The Major-Domo did not especially care. Greeting those called to visit the Queen's private office was quite the most tedious aspect of his job. He let his face sink into its most neutral expression.

The tailor sighed disconsolately. "It's just that I'd been waiting for so long for this..." he managed, finally, letting the folds of fabric on his arm fall to the floor, a perfect metaphor for his defeat.

The Major-Domo looked down at the crumpled pile of cloth. "You seem to have *dropped* something. Kindly retrieve it and then the First Underbutler will show you out." He smiled his most official, officious, insincere smile.

Happily, fallacious sincerity was a required skill at Court, and the Sir Tancred Golightly, Chief Steward and Major Domo, was a master.

The man smiled back, the kind of hopeful, pathetic smile suppliants to Court seemed to believe would win the day. It didn't. He snatched up his fallen cloth and left with his tail, and some of his cloth, between his legs.

Tancred watched the tailor leave. It was not the man's fault, he supposed. He checked himself for feeling undue sympathy towards a *tradesman*, albeit one of the few accorded 'By Appointment…' status. He glanced at his exquisitely crafted fob watch and then up at the Imperial Clock which stood high above a fountain of dolphins, unicorns and one wistful looking mermaid at the far end of the vaulted hallway.

Watch and clock were precisely synchronised, as it should be.

The tailor had been predictably late, a cardinal sin within the confines of the Palace but only to be expected outside the radiance of timepieces set to Imperial Time. The man would be working to English Proper Time, the inferior brand of time which marked out the middle classes.

That Imperial Time might cost the clothier a year's income to acquire and maintain was *not* the Major-Domo's concern. The man should simply have arrived a little earlier but had, with typical bourgeois complacency, trusted that his own time was of sufficiency. Tancred had, of course, anticipated the man's late arrival as well as the abrupt cancellation of the appointment. He had ample time.

Imperial Time was indeed a precious commodity and it ensured that Tancred, and everyone else in the Palace, would be where they were supposed to be at exactly the correct time, all the time.

In the Palace, everything – but *everything* – worked like clockwork.

Tancred made his way up the left staircase by the fountain and along the Hall of Heroes, a cavalcade of portraits, statuary and military paraphernalia which rippled its way from the Grand Lobby to the Great Corridor, off of which all the most important functions of the Palace took place. Ordinarily, he would take the opportunity to savour this spectacular celebration of the founders of the Empire of Centuries, but today he was burdened by a concern which occupied the majority of his waking thoughts and which perturbed his sleep to boot: the declining health of Her Imperial Majesty.

It had been his honour – surely not the right word but how else might one describe such an unexpected intimacy? – to have witnessed the very commencement of this strange illness a few days before.

ΨΨΨΨΨΨ

On that inauspicious Wednesday, the Major-Domo had conducted Her Majesty to a meeting of her top diplomats, where she was due to lead a discussion on the Mid-Eastern Colonies, in particular to decide upon the eventual fate of the Grand Engine at Inkerman. The infernal machine had become a source of worry for the military and politicians alike, having seemingly taken on a life of its own and resisting any attempts to deactivate it. It was now on the brink of causing a diplomatic scandal, so the Palace had become involved. Her Majesty's diplomats and engineers would advise her, naturally, but the final decision as to the correct course of action would be hers alone. Such had protocol been since she ascended to the throne, such it was intended to be for as long as Her Majesty felt able, which everyone in the court firmly believed would be *in perpetuity*.

Her Majesty had been her usual courteous self on the walk to the Great Room at the heart of the palace where these conclaves occurred. She enquired, as usual, on the health of the Major-Domo's family, his own health and had asked some general questions aimed at ascertaining the mood of the citizenry in general.

Tancred found this part of his function taxing to say the least. He did not have a family (and had never had one), was in poor health (but would never trouble Her Majesty with such personal nonsense) and, having rarely left the palace in the last twenty years, had not the foggiest clue as to the mood of the citizenry. There were whole governmental agencies devoted to measuring, monitoring and, if necessary, correcting the mood of the citizenry, but he had not the slightest interest in their functions nor the outcomes. As ever, he would smile, mouth pleasantries and impart the little scraps of London gossip he overheard from time to time in the kitchens or the butlers' pantries, and that was that.

As they moved through the glass walkway over the Inner Orchards, the sunlight had suddenly blazed from behind a cloud, causing him to sneeze fulsomely, and embarrassingly. The Queen stopped, as did he.

Her Majesty was most solicitous, looking up at him with gentle enquiry. He apologised and wiped his eyes, feeling a small prick of discomfort as a fragment of dried mucus he had not succeeded in flannelling off that morning pulled out an eyelash with it.

He apologised again, whereupon Her Majesty smiled tightly, as was her custom, and they quickly regained their progress.

They entered the Great Room to find the usual assemblage of diplomats, generals, admirals, governors and adjutants, all clad in bright worsted twill coats each sporting a dazzling array of medal ribbons, silk sashes, twisted cord epaulettes, brass buttons and so on. Tancred often fought hard to suppress laughter at this point due to the sheer overabundance of honours on display. Had the Army or Navy even fought that many battles? What could all these medals possibly be for? It had once occurred to him that these men looked like nothing more than a parade of expensive parrots and he had almost cracked a rib trying not to guffaw. The echo of that supressed belch of hilarity often threatened, but not this day, for some reason.

First, Her Majesty's speech became a little slurred, turning the 's' of Mombasa into 'sh'. Most unfortunate. Nobody reacted, of course, but the next sentence brought another instance and by the fourth instance, the Head of the Diplomatic Corps had, with extravagant politeness, suggested the meeting might be more profitably concluded at another time. Inkerman could wait.

Tancred had conducted Her Majesty to her chambers, whereupon her maids took charge. He was relieved to hand her over to her personal staff, but now worried.

Those worries compounded in the next few days.

"I've never seen anything like this." Her Majesty's chief Lady-In-Waiting dabbed delicately at her exquisite pink lips. She and the Major-Domo took tea twice a week in the Lace Arboretum.

Tancred plopped two of the tiny sugar cubes into his cup of Darjeeling. "What do you mean, Countess?"

The Lady Margaret, Countess of Stroud, smiled delicately at his courtly refusal to address her by her first name, albeit that they were what one might term intimate confidants. "At first it seemed only to be a few words, mispronounced. And then Her Majesty began missing words altogether. Soon, her speech, which had become somewhat infrequent, deteriorated into an incomprehensible babble. Then, yesterday, she stopped speaking altogether."

"Why was I not informed of this earlier?" said Tancred, but in a kindly tone, without reproach.

"I did not want to trouble your good self with it, Tancred." She touched his hand briefly. "You have so much to concern yourself with, managing the palace and whatnot."

He felt himself flush at the touch and at the use of his first name. "Thank you for your kindness, but Her Imperial Majesty's health is without equal the most important consideration for us here in the palace and throughout the Empire."

The Countess blushed.

He shook his head and smiled warmly. This was his sincere smile, though he secretly worried some might not be able to perceive the difference between this and his professional, insincere one. It was of the greatest importance to him that the Countess of Stroud did *not* misapprehend him. "It is of no matter. You are informing me now."

The Countess smiled but then her expression turned to one of worry. "Her movement has also decreased. She has been bed-bound for two days now."

"And the good Herr Doktor?"

"Summoned yesterday, although he could not at first be reached. He is on his way post-haste from his summer residence in Banbury."

"Ah."

"I should like you to be there, Tancred."

"Really? I…"

"I know you consider this a very delicate matter, and so do I. But I do feel it would do well to have another man in attendance when the good Herr Doktor is examining Her Majesty."

He gulped. "Very well. I will of course be there, Countess."

She beamed, and placed her hand on his once again, with a slightly heavier touch this time. "Oh, thank you, Tancred, thank you."

He blushed again, more deeply this time.

"She is, after all…" The Countess dipped her other hand for another cucumber sandwich, "…our Forever Queen."

ᛟᛟᛟᛟᛟᛟ

The Coronation of Her Majesty Queen Alexandrina Victoria as Forever Queen had been an "event which scales the very highest imaginable heights of the British Empire", according to *The London Times*, a phrase which had struck Tancred as peculiar at the time given that once one had scaled the tallest mountain, where was there to go but down?

This Empire of Centuries was, it was to be acknowledged, in good shape. Its multifarious colonies were happy and prosperous, any thought of rebellion banished to dark whispers in the darkest sewers, although it seemed the Fifteen Colonies had become somewhat restive of late. Neither Army nor Navy had suffered a defeat in twenty years and had not lost a real war in two hundred. Great Britain dominated global trade, and defined culture and style throughout the civilised world. Her manufactured goods were the backbone of civilisation, her machines without parallel.

The remarkable, untroubled progress of this Third Age of Empire was put down to Her Majesty's extraordinary lease on life. The physically tiny monarch had survived – some might say 'endured' – fully sixteen Prime Ministers and, once she had achieved a usefully regal countenance, had not aged. She wore the same outfit each day, except on Christmas Day and when Parliament was to be opened. Her hair remained bright white, her eyes were still clear blue jewels and her mouth only ever deviated from a straight line when she brought down the first grouse of summer on whichever of her Scottish Estates had the honour of hosting the Royal Hunt that year. She was on every banknote, every stamp and countless statues, from Singapore to New York, Cape Town to Edinburgh.

As long as she endured, the Empire endured.

But as awe-inspiring as it might be, the Major-Domo knew full-well that the Empire was a most complex machine. There were so many moving parts, so many operators, so much which could, potentially, go wrong. It was impossible to keep every aspect of it under such detailed supervision so as to avert trouble, impossible to monitor every grain of rice in the warehouses, to keep an eye on every soldier, functionary, servant, lackey. In such a delicate engine, the smallest thing could cause upset.

If Her Majesty were ever to… he did not want to think about *that* day.

If it ever came.

She was the Forever Queen, after all.

And in the Empire, titles meant something.

ΨΨΨΨΨΨ

He was shown into the vestibule adjacent to the Royal Bedchamber and waited quietly while one of the girls fetched tea. She returned only minutes later with a small pot of Lapsang and a rack laden with Punch Fancies, Genoa Tartlets and Russian Sandwiches. Tancred's mouth watered, but he dared not indulge, lest he create crumbs which might spoil his attire.

He was saved a moment later when the Countess, clad in a white felt gown, gloves and mobcap and wearing a white gauze mask, bade him enter. Immediately inside the door was a semi-circular cordon of white chiffon curtains which rose from floor to ceiling. Through the curtains he could see four white-clad figures, the bulkiest clearly the form of the good Herr Doktor. The Countess offered Tancred a gown, mask, gloves and white rubber overslippers. He dressed quickly, the Countess inspected him and, ensuring the door was closed and sealed behind him, drew back the curtains.

As they moved towards the bed, the good Herr Doktor turned around. "Ah, good. I believe I have managed to identify the source of the malady." He bade them come closer to the bed, and his three assistants parted to reveal the Sovereign of the Empire of Centuries.

The Queen lay on the bed in the most indelicate pose, which caused Tancred to flush deepest red in embarrassment. The Countess seemed equally shocked, but quickly regained her poise and smiled at him from behind her mask, causing the most delightful wrinkles around her eyes. This had something of a calming effect, but his eyes were drawn quickly back to Her Imperial Majesty.

The Queen was on her back, her head tipped back, staring into space. Her arms were flung to either side, hands clawing the bedclothes as if to provide some stability. Her legs were – what was that colonial expression, *akimbo*? Each was bent at a ninety-degree angle from the knee, splayed apart like a frog on a dissecting table, feet turned out. Her pelvis was raised slightly, forcing him to look directly into her most intimate region.

That too, was wide open, the rubber lips prised apart and held by brass clamps.

The good Herr Doktor brought a rosewood switch with a pointed silver tip to bear as if it were a sword and poked it into the Queen's gaping nethers. "You see, *here*? That is an unacceptable build-up of grease…" He took a white cloth from one of his assistants and delicately wiped the inside of each rubber lip, pushing the resulting swab towards the Major-Domo and the Countess. "Unacceptable!"

"It smells…fishy," said Tancred, reddening further and feeling distinctly warm in his various layers.

"So," acknowledged the good Herr Doktor. "It is my proprietary blend of liver oils from the Black Sea Sturgeon, the Scottish River Salmon und the Hairy Dogger Flatfish."

The Countess snickered.

The good Herr Doktor fixed her with a dark stare.

"Oh," said Tancred. "And that's good is it?"

"Typically, yes." The good Herr Doktor tapped the Queen's metal pubis. "The oils are perfect lubrication for all fine systems, but if any foreign object should find its way into the system, anything can happen."

"And some did?" said the Countess.

"*Kommen sie mit mir.*" The good Herr Doktor trailed the rosewood switch from the pubis over the lower abdomen towards the gaping ribcage. The brass ribs were individually articulated and had all been pushed to their furthest outward extent, revealing the impossibly intricate machine within, a mass of highly polished alloys, shining with jewels.

"Gosh, so many jewels…" The Countess trailed off. Jewellery was, famously, one of her peccadilloes.

"*Genau,*" said the good Herr Doktor. "They reduce friction." He shook his head to get himself back on track. "You see here?" He pointed the switch towards the centre of the machinery where a small hexagonal box lay, surrounded by a spaghetti of slim silver wires. The good Herr Doktor tapped on the box, which was oozing a yellow liquid. "This is the main interlock for the pressure lubri-cant system." He sighed heavily. "I did recommend this chamber be *larger* and for the whole system to be assisted by pneumatics, but your so-called engineers said it would mean Her Majesty *veezed*, und they considered it unac-ceptable. Und so, they designed *this*. Und presto, we have a malfunction!"

"Do you know what caused it? Can she be repaired?" asked the Major-Domo.

The good Herr Doktor laughed heartily behind his mask. "Oh, for sure I know what caused this *fehlfunktion*." He motioned to one of his assistants who handed him a small kidney bowl. He held it out for them to see. At the centre of the bowl was a small smear of the yellow gunk.

"What are we looking at?" said the Countess.

The good Herr Doktor sighed exasperatedly and made a frantic motion to the other assistant, who handed him a pair of complicated-looking goggles, such as one might find at a fine optician. "*Schau mal!*" He waved the bowl from side to side, inviting inspection.

The Countess placed the leather harness of the gog-gles over her mobcap, and the good Herr Doktor flipped all the lenses into place. She flinched suddenly. "Gosh!" She peered nervously into the kidney bowl. "Oh…yes, I see. Good gracious, you mean all this trouble was caused by that?" She removed the goggles, offered them to the Major-Domo.

"*Genau.*"

"What caused all this trouble?" The Major-Domo took the goggles from the Countess and made to put them on.

"My dear fellow." The good Herr Doktor snatched the

goggles. "It was an eyelash, plus some attendant, well, other *matter*," he said, with the derision of a master engineer finding his excavation machine clogged by errant swarf.

"Good grief." The Major-Domo thought immediately of his sneeze, how he had wiped his eyes, turned as the Queen – short as she was – had looked up to him. He felt himself flush once again.

"Quite," said the good Herr Doktor. "It is only to be expected. With such a complex und delicate machine, it is only a matter of time before it breaks down. Happily, we can maintain it for some time to come but eventually it will go *kaput*. Everything does. Nothing, my friend, *nothing* is forever."

He looked back, then, at the Queen, spatchcocked on the bed, ready for her winding key, and it hit him. It all hit him, at once, as if he had plunged into the Serpentine in Winter.

He turned to the Countess. "Margaret. I love you."

She blushed, deep crimson, with delightful wrinkles at the eyes.

"Ah," said the good Herr Doktor. "*Carpe diem*, eh?" He laughed gently, placing an arm around each of them, bringing them together.

THE END

ΨΨΨΨΨΨ

Thank you so much for taking the time to read *Colossus of the Thames and Other Tales* – I hope you enjoyed it!

I'd very much value your feedback, so if you have time to write a review on Amazon, I'd be very grateful.

Alternatively, you can send me feedback or questions directly on Twitter – @authorbear2 – or email me: mark@typhon-creative.com. You can also contact me via my website – www.typhon-creative.com where you can subscribe to my newsletter, for news, updates and offers, including an exclusive **subscriber-only short story**.

Final thanks to ...

Katherine, my editor, for her superb input and eagle eye.

Pete, for his amazing cover art, and Euan for his invaluable help with design and production.

Harry, for all his support, encouragement and special help with 'The Secrets of Art'.

DT, for giving me the kick up the arse I sorely needed, and for taking the time to read my stuff and give his thoughts.

ΨΨΨΨΨΨ

Coming soon...

THE ARMAMENTARIUM

A STEAMPUNK NOVEL

When a massive explosion sinks the battleship *HMS Adamant* in the River Thames during the visit of Queen Alexandrina Victoria, The Forever Queen, the Government blames Radical terrorists and begins a terrifying crackdown.

But Paul Royall Ciardi, reporter on London's best-selling popular daily newspaper, *The Star and Globe*, is not so sure. How did terrorists manage to smuggle huge amounts of explosives onto a Royal Navy ship? And where did they get them in the first place?

Ciardi taps his best source in the military, Bertie Palk, who works at The Armamentarium, the centre of military research and development for the Empire of Great Britain, the Fifteen Colonies and the Good Hope. But Palk isn't talking, and Ciardi's curiosity is about to get him embroiled in a deadly plot which could change the whole world…

ΨΨΨΨΨΨ

Typhon-Creative Ltd
www.typhon-creative.com

NOTES

A few historical notes for readers.

Floriography (The Flower Girls)

Floriography – the cryptological communication of information via the use of flowers – is an ancient art and was popular in Victorian times in courtship rituals. A girl would wear a bloom to signify to her lover if she wished him to approach, to leave, to delay and so on. Each type of flower, and very often different colours of the same type, had individual meanings, usually a single word ('Delay' etc). I adapted this for 'The Flower Girls', and all the meanings of flowers in the story are taken from one of the many dictionaries on the topic.

Pneumatic Trains (various stories)

We're all familiar with the London Underground (the Tube), but when inventors started developing complex engineering during the Industrial Revolution, some became entranced by the possibilities of pneumatics, a branch of science relying on the use of gases or compressed air in pressurised environments, enabling the generation of great force. In 1799, Londoner George Medhurst proposed moving goods pneumatically through cast iron tubes, and in 1812 proposed using the same principles for passenger carriages. Various inventors experimented with test lines. Then in 1834, the 'Dalkey Atmospheric Railway' was installed as an extension to the Dublin and Kingstown Railway, using traction pipes fitted in the centre of the tracks. This inspired the French to use a similar system to conquer a daunting incline on the St Germain line, where steam engines were not powerful to pull (or push) a train. In England, the London & Croydon line also used traction line technology. With the advent of more powerful steam locomotives, pneumatic technology fell out of use.

Time as a commodity (various stories)

We take access to reliable timekeeping for granted these days, but in the Victorian era this was not the case. The vast majority of the population could not afford reliable pendulum clocks or less accurate pocket watches (men) or wristwatches (women) and in any case, all clocks needed to be corrected where possible. Liverpool – the busiest port in the world at the time – was the first British city to formulate a system for synchronising clocks, in the 1840s. The Greenwich Observatory in London became the centre of official time and would send out men to deliver time to the government offices in London, a method which would be superseded by telegraph distribution of the correct time. When one of these men, John Belville, died in 1856, his wife Maria proposed to the Observatory that she might carry on the service privately, taking the service to the ordinary folk of London. Her daughter, Ruth – who became quite famous due to legal action against her by a telegraph company – continued selling time until 1939.

Dreadnought (Battleship Junk)

HMS Dreadnought was a British battleship, launched in 1906. Her revolutionary features included "all big gun" armament and steam turbines, immediately outclassing pretty much anything afloat. She was so much of a game changer she gave her name to battleships designed after her, and all the battleships then in service became known as pre-dreadnoughts. Her appearance caused a naval arms race which lasted until the advent of WWI. Though not strictly a Victorian invention by the time she came out, her innovations were in train while Victoria was still on the throne.

The Fifteen Colonies (Antebellum, and mentioned in other stories)

The original British foothold in America was known as the Thirteen Colonies. These colonies declared independence from the British crown in 1776. In my steampunk world, America has not united but remains the province of the various European superpowers of the day. Britain holds the Fifteen Colonies, essentially most of the Eastern Seaboard of the modern-day United States. Kentucky, where 'Antebellum' is set, was not one of the original Thirteen Colonies but a county of Virginia (which was). Kentucky was admitted into the United States as the fifteenth state in 1792.

"In his house at R'lyeh, dead Cthulhu lies dreaming..." (The Lost Poets)

This line is a quote from the seminal 'Call of Cthulhu', by H P Lovecraft, which was published in the American magazine *Weird Tales* in 1928. I have been a fan of the works of H P Lovecraft – the granddaddy of cosmic horror – since I was a kid, and his works and those of other authors featuring the Cthulhu Mythos, as it has come to be known, have grown steadily more popular as time has gone on. I wanted to feature a few hints of horror in this collection (see also 'The Night Doctor', 'The Button Man' and 'The Unruly Cuckoo Clock') to hint that behind all the amazing technology and social tension of my steampunk London, an even darker storyline is building. Watch this space...

Lightning Source UK Ltd.
Milton Keynes UK
UKHW010735051021
391704UK00002B/335